THE ONE

Activation

j. manoa

EPIC
Press

Activation
The One: Book #6

Written by J. Manoa

Copyright © 2016 by Abdo Consulting Group, Inc.

Published by EPIC Press™
PO Box 398166
Minneapolis, MN 55439

Cover design by Candice Keimig
Images for cover art obtained from iStockPhoto.com
Edited by Ryan Hume

Library of Congress Cataloging-in-Publication Data

Manoa, J.
Activation / J. Manoa.
p. cm. — (The one; #6)
Summary: After demonstrating Solar Flare's destruction and leaving Odin
completely powerless, Wendell has won. His plan is progressing exactly as he said it
would—making the world everything he wants it to be. With his home taken away
and only Dr. Burnett left from the life he once had, only one purpose remains for
Odin: revenge.
ISBN 978-1-68076-055-2 (hardcover)
1. Imaginary playmates—Fiction. 3. Interpersonal relations—Fiction.
4. Secrets—Fiction. 5. Psychic ability—Fiction. 6. Revenge—Fiction.
7. Young adult fiction. I. Title.
[Fic]—dc23
2015949422

EPIC
Press

EPICPRESS.COM

To Hawaii,
Your brother misses you

1

I WAS LYING UNDER THE OAK TREE IN THE BACK YARD that afternoon, admiring how the sun broke through the gaps between the leaves and the branches, and the wind pushing them back and forth. The dark and the light fluctuated in waves that crashed into my eyes. It was amazing that light would travel so far, from the sun to me, only to be blocked at the very end of the journey by a tiny leaf or a twig. Even the most powerful energy could be stopped.

My favorite place that summer was out there. The grass was warm in the sun, a pleasant warmth, better than on the sidewalk or the road, and cool in the shade. Going between the two of them was like moving through seasons in seconds. I'd lay out in the sun, flat on my back, face up and eyes closed, until I'd begin to feel my skin burning. Then I'd relocate to the spot of grass between two forking roots. What was warm and impossibly bright was now cool and with a light that seemed to dance. At times the sun was gone, at times it was stunning. I never knew which it would be, or when, but knew it would change.

It was also the only place where I ever felt as though no one else from the house was watching.

Can you feel it, Odin?

I knew he wasn't really there but I still liked to imagine him, sitting against the trunk of the oak tree, picking grass, or drawing pictures in the dirt. He sounded just like me. He looked just like me, or maybe a little smaller. He had the same colored eyes and hair, the same plain cheeks and forehead, but none of the details, shadows and lines that come with age, like back when we were both unformed.

It was nice having someone familiar. He was the last familiar thing left from the time—it had been nearly a year—since the accident. Everyone called it an accident.

"What?" I said aloud, despite knowing the only voice I heard was in my head.

The world turning.

"No." That's one of the things we learned that year, movement of planets. The teacher, Mrs. Roth, used an old globe to demonstrate the rotation. During recess some of the other boys in the class would spin the globe as fast as they could while telling another, Justin, his name was, that if they spun the globe too quickly everyone on the planet would fly off.

It never stops. It just turns and turns and turns.

"I know."

I heard that if you stand still you can feel the world turn.

"That's dumb," I said, squinting as the sun reappeared in the still air.

His laugh was a gentle shake in my mind. A vibration that tickled almost to my fingers.

"It's so big and we're so small," I said. "How would we know?"

It's not as big as we think.

I liked to imagine him in school, never in class but during lunch and recess, when I'd usually sit by myself or wait for the other kids to finish on the swings. He told me not to talk to him around other people because it would make them want to talk to him too, and he didn't want to talk to them. He wanted to talk only to me.

Do you like it here?

"It's good."

I like it too. It's better than the other place.

I didn't really remember home, the apartment where I used to live with my parents, my other parents. I remembered that we had a window that faced a wall with a pipe stuck out of it and sometimes there would be water leaking out from the end. There was some writing on the side of the pipe that I couldn't read. I remember the exit of the building and Jerry talking to my mom and dad. I don't remember crying after the accident. People were very sad when they talked to me. They told me they were sorry and that I could cry and be sad, but not to worry. They would make sure I was safe.

Maybe it was because I didn't know them very well, Mom and Dad. I couldn't picture the details on their faces, the shadows and lines, they were also blank. They were there and then they were gone and someone else was there. Then someone else and someone else. And then I was here and new people were telling me to call them Mom and Dad, so I did because they were about the same age, and were doing the same things. I knew something really bad had happened, something I knew I shouldn't look back on, but it felt like everything was still okay. It felt like nothing had been lost. It just wasn't there anymore.

I think I should stay here.

"Me too," I said. I sat up and slapped as far as I could reach on my back to knock the grass off. I'd spent enough time in the shade. It was time to go back into the light.

We can make this world better.

"Can you feel it, Odin?"

He descends the steps from the heart of the machine. The vibration has stopped, the spinning slowed to inertia only, and the metallic scream lowered to low hum. The machine's light blinks as it powers down, like the sun through waving leaves.

Burnett remains collapsed on her knees, head down, shoulders hunched, knuckles on the ground between her legs. A tree stump is stuck in the floor, useless but not enough of a bother to remove.

Wendell's footfalls reverberate in the hollow metal before he reaches the solid bottom. He looks at me, head tilted back, hands lifting upwards. He glances skyward and then back to me.

"Could you feel their lives end? The energy disappear? Tens of thousands of lights vanishing from the world?"

He must be bluffing. What I saw was one possibility. The images: faces of George and Rose, the dust cloud over flat land, the woman in the rubble, the skyline through Burnett's office window, my school, Eden—both the girl and the world—most of these don't exist. Haven't for years. They were visions of other worlds. The light above the school, it was another possibility. Another of the unreal things—past and present—which came into my head. It must have been that and nothing more. Nothing real.

"No?" He stops. His hands and scrawny arms

drop to his sides, as though in disappointment. "Maybe that is because there is nothing to feel."

My legs burn holding me up. My left arm aches. My right has a sharp stab from a torn muscle in the upper arm. At least I can move my hands under the metal pieces jammed into the wall, but any pressure at the forearms or elbows just pushes against the restraints. I can't do anything. Even the blood barely moves down my forearms.

I could get out of here if I had my powers. I might not be able to move myself, but I could move other things. The closest I've gotten is feeling him connect through me, a conduit, an extension cord into the energy source. The images must have been a figment of his imagination, the same as in the bowling alley, or floating down a road with vehicles parting and eyes glowing. It was one among infinite possibilities.

He moves to within a few steps away from me. "Physical law says that energy cannot be created or destroyed," he says. "So where does that energy go?" I could try to kick him, but that would do nothing. "That energy, in the minds and bodies of those people when they suddenly cease to be? Is it all lost?"

I feel the muscles in my cheeks flex. I used to like the way that looked, like a lion staring back in the mirror.

"How about you, Doctor?" He speaks to Burnett's rounded back. "You are supposed to be the expert on the mind. Can you explain that?"

She is silent. She doesn't move or twitch or anything.

"Nothing," he says, turning back to me. "Maybe that is it. No great surge of energy—of life force pouring out into the universe—just nothing. The world goes on. Yes, the people will panic, but eventually . . . " He stares blankly for a moment. "It is starting right now. I can see it all. Breaking news and videos feeds. Shock and terror and disbelief."

"You're sick," I growl.

"I am how you made me, Odin. No more sick than you."

"And I'm supposed to believe you? Just take your word for it?"

"It does not matter what you believe. Reality is reality, whether you acknowledge it or not."

"You're lying."

"No, Odin. They lied!" he snaps. He stabs a bony finger in Burnett's direction. "They lied every morning when you woke up in that house to captors who told you they were guardians. They lied in every repeated refrain of responsibility and trust." It's one of the only times I can remember where he's shown emotion. "They lied in saying that everything they did, programming you into trusting them, stealing your powers for themselves, was somehow for the good of all humanity. They lied, Odin! They want to deny what the world truly is." He straightens himself. "I want to make the world what it should be."

My teeth press together so hard I feel it in my

gums. Even with the other burning, relentless pains from legs to neck, I feel this one. Maybe because it's voluntary or because I want it to be noticed, but it's there.

"You should be glad that they did not suffer. Not when they died, at least."

"Fuck you!" I lurch forward. The metal curves tug at my flesh. The trickles of blood on my arms feel cool against the flaring nerves under the skin. I kick one foot out. It doesn't reach him. Nowhere close. I fling my wrists and fingers in his direction. I roll my shoulders side to side. Skin tears with my move. I want to rip him apart with my bare hands. I want to dig my fingers into his eyes. I want to shred his face apart like paper. I want to hear his bones pop. Break them slowly. I cringe as a fire ignites in my arm, a blaze in my shoulder. I want to hold his still beating heart in my hands. I want to show it to him as the last thing he ever sees. I want him to suffer.

"You," he says, "need to calm down."

I feel the metal arches pinning me to the wall dig in farther. Fresh dust rises and concrete crumbs fall off the sloping end. There's a pinch at the point of contact between the wall, the metal, and my forearms. I scream at him, feral and vicious.

"So much effort," he says, staring at me, large flakes of skin hanging around his nostrils, lips, and brows, "on something pointless."

I bare my teeth in anger, pain, exhaustion, frustration, desperation. I want to bite his face off.

"You cannot do anything to help them anymore. Not that you ever could."

I thrust my shoulder forward. A muted pop shakes through my arm. I shout, kick, flail, stomp. I roar at his face. It all does nothing.

He presses me against the wall, feet out and flat as though nailed to the ground. The pain in my arm makes my teeth grit. Drops of blood roll down each forearm. He grabs my face in his palm. I snap my teeth at him. He pushes my head back.

One finger bends my nose. Another presses my eye.

"You do not believe me," he says. He exhales loudly in my ear. His voice is a needle stabbing on every word. "I am stronger than you. I will make you understand."

There's a shock in the middle of my skull. Then images and sounds come at once, a surge of energy into my head.

———⌣———

I see screams and lights, and a dust cloud so heavy it's almost solid. I hear a woman shouting, "Oh god! Oh no!" I see a lake with a skyline view that disappears in a blink. "Reports coming in . . . " says a man in a leather jacket pointing at the huge plume. " . . . It happened just moments ago . . . " There are sirens and flashing lights from several dozen police cars unloading cops in gas masks carrying riot shields. A highway is closed off to traffic. Barricades hold back cars and a throng of screaming, crying people between them.

"Clear the area! Emergency personnel only! We need to get through!"

A brown-haired woman in a raincoat holding a microphone with a *News 8* logo and a white cloth just off her nose and mouth says in a voice pitched high with adrenaline and astonishment, "On the scene—" Police hold people back behind her. A wall of ash-gray dust billows into sight. "—seemed centered on the town of Clarke outside of—" She coughs violently as the dust cloud blows across. The crowd shields its eyes, noses, and mouths. "See," she struggles into the mic, "whole town covered," coughs again, "thick cloud of dust." One cop rushes to shove the camera away. A light layer of gray dust descends like powder upon the barricade, the police, the cars, and the people who abandoned them.

"Back in your vehicles!" the officer in the

gas mask yells. "Emergency personnel can't get through!"

"Goddamn jihadists," someone in the crowd says.

"As you can see," the reporter says between coughs, "there's panic out here."

"Let me through!"

"My family is—"

The whole crowd shifts sideways as police behind shields push it aside, splitting the horde like a tanker plowing through the ocean. A white van slowly advances between the two sides of the parting crowd.

Do you see it, Odin?

His voice lingers behind the images, like they did before, when he was in my head. The same way vibrations formed Eden's words.

Across the lake, the wind has shifted, blowing the dust toward the highway on the other side of town. In its place is nothing. There were buildings. Now there is emptiness. Sobs and screams fill the air. Eyes are wild with panic and disbelief. The city and the area around it has completely vanished.

Can you feel it?

The white van stops as the road becomes too hard to drive through. The ground is piled thick with loose rocks. People in hazmat suits unload from the back of the van. They continue on foot where wheels can't go. One of them is a small woman with her suit bunched in the back. She keeps one arm extended. Her hand is only feet away yet almost invisible in the mass of dust that surrounds her. She steps cautiously over the shifting rock chunks and shattered road. Everything beneath her is reduced to pebbles and ash. There are not even the large piles of rubble typically left behind in a war zone. Ahead is nothing but dust, no shadows of buildings or standing walls. Flat land is the only thing in sight and nothing else. The rocks shift and she stumbles. She catches herself before falling. She glances down to see her gloved hand covered in blood. She holds her palm out in front of her, not close enough to see much, but close enough to see something. Thick drops fall back to the ground. She shakes her bloody hand frantically. She waves it around like she could fling the blood off. She keeps her hand extended and kneels down to see where the blood came from, waving the dust away as best as she can.

This is the world now.

Blood-soaked fabric. Mashed meat stuck to bone splinters.

This is not a possibility.

She recoils. She bumps into another person in a hazmat suit. They steady each other. The other one, a man, startles to see her blood-covered hand.

This is the truth.

There is a clearing in the dust ahead. There are crushed rocks and broken metal and blood. Everything is low and flat. Crushed. All that rises is dust.

"Do you see it now?" Wendell says. His fingertips press into my face. Thin bolts of pressure force my head against the wall.

"Do you believe me now, Odin? Do you finally see the world as it is?" He curls his fingers to dig his nails in. "Now they know. Now they can see. This is how it begins." He gives a last shove before scratching his hand down. His jagged nails leave stinging trails across my face. "Soon they will all see. They will all know." He steps away. His skin is almost as gray as the ash and dust blanketing my city. "Then they will beg for it to end. They will do anything to survive."

A shock begins in the center of my head, shooting through every part of my brain and then to the rest of my body. I twitch uncontrollably. One leg stretches out, shaking. The back of my head bounces against the wall. Every other pain fades. It feels like I'm about to explode, like I've grabbed onto power lines and can't let go. I don't want to let go.

"Now we let the panic take over," he says, drifting toward Burnett, who is slouched on her knees. "We let them rip themselves apart like the animals they are." He pats the hair on Burnett's head. She flinches to the side and mutters something, the first sign of life I've seen from her in far too long. "It's not real," she says.

I can see it, in the past, a second ago. I can see her face, eyes closed but not squeezed, the little bit of extra skin hanging from her cheeks making her face appear puffier than usual. I can freeze the image of her in my mind, rotate it, zoom, see the cracks in Wendell's fingers as they reach for her head, see myself behind them, looking at their backs, pinned against the wall. I can see everything.

It must have been the contact with him, the anomaly, him physically implanting the images into my mind. It must have re-established my connection with the energy. It's as though he left some piece of him behind, and it activated that place in my brain, the posterior cingular cortex, the dark energy region, opening the chan—

It doesn't matter how it happened, it only matters that it happened. All that matters. All matter.

"It is too bad you cannot share in this moment as well, Doctor. Tragic that after everything you did, everything you gave up, you cannot witness this triumph." He looks up, into the computer station, then to the machine. "Maybe there is another way." Wendell breaks into a stride toward the machine, the weapon. His weapon.

"It's not real," Burnett mutters.

An unseen force hit it from above. The entire city, from downtown to the suburbs, smashed into the ground. It was over in a flash. Literally. Like lightning. Nothing was blown outward, only down.

The woman in the hazmat suit continues her search as more bubbles of clear air appear in the dense cloud of dust and ash. It's hard to tell where she is exactly without the buildings or street signs. She comes upon a pile of much larger rubble that ends at the ground. Must be the basement of one of the tall buildings downtown. The upper floors are now all shoved into the subterranean area, the same streets I used to look down upon from Burnett's office. The sidewalk has fallen into the sewer pipe trenches beneath the streets. Compacted masses slope gently where other buildings were. Pedestrians . . . it's like they've been popped, or squashed like ants from some giant hand. They always looked so small through that window.

Other emergency crews are wandering through now. EMTs on foot and police and fire fighters in oxygen masks are coughing with rags over their mouths, crouching as they walk, staring at the places where the road collapsed, at the blood seeping between the cracks. An officer, his name is Sanders, looks into one of the partially-filled building basements. It's several floors deep and filled almost to the very top. Through the big chunks of matter, he sees a hand with curled fingers. It belongs to a woman with light hair draped across her face, her eyes open, staring upward. A tear in her shirt exposes her shoulder just above the spot where the concrete slab fell on top of her.

Marcus Richard Sanders is an eight-year veteran of the police department. I don't know him, know nothing at all, but can see him. See his life. All of it.

His first day included two calls: one animal-abuse complaint that turned out to just be a barking dog chained in the garage because the owner had no other way to control it, and one domestic disturbance that resulted in he and his partner having a shotgun turned on them through the front door. They arrested the husband for violating the terms of his parole.

The husband, Neil Miller, was the manager of a kitchenware store in the mall. He met his wife, Lisa, during a summer when she worked there while finishing her paralegal degree. They had a son named Nicholas who died of leukemia when he was twelve years old. It was a few months later when they had their first major argument.

I can see it all.

I see Neil and Lisa, people I've never known, sitting at his hospital bed. I see them yelling at each other from across the apartment. I see Sanders and his partner Murphy taking Neil away in handcuffs.

Lisa is in San Diego now. She moved there five years ago to work for a different firm after her divorce from Neil, who tried to stay in the city before seeking a fresh start in Jacksonville. He stares at the television in the two-bedroom apartment he shares with his girlfriend and her daughter.

They are clearer in my head than any strangers have ever been before.

On Neil's television screen is a mass of dust rising from the ground, slowly tilting in the wind. "No video yet but reports still coming in of a flash over the area," says Edward Michaels, an NBC news reporter. His life is open to me, too. I know it is. "Witnesses say when the light was gone all that remained was . . . well, you can see what remains."

There is a jolt, there, in the center of my head. It's a spark that I feel jump from behind my right eye to my left ear. I can see them: Marcus, Lisa, Neil, Edward. People I have never met and never known. Every one of their experiences are on display in front of me, like movies I can watch, rewind, pause, and move through. It feels like my head is pushing against the inside of my skull. This energy, it is dying to be released.

***

Wendell leans closer to the machine. He rubs at a scratch that could be a crack. Burnett rocks back and forth, staring at her hands on the floor. She repeats, "It's not real. It's not real."

I can barely move my fingers under the sides of metal shells pining me to the lowered entrance wall. The arches are embedded so deep their slope is barely visible, like that of the world itself, what we see of it. I can't even use my entire right arm. I can't feel it move. My head is pounding. Must be several hundred pounds of metal holding me here.

Don't think. Make it happen.

"Doctor," I say.

She rocks, whispering to herself.

"Doctor Burnett," I say again.

She turns to me.

"Move."

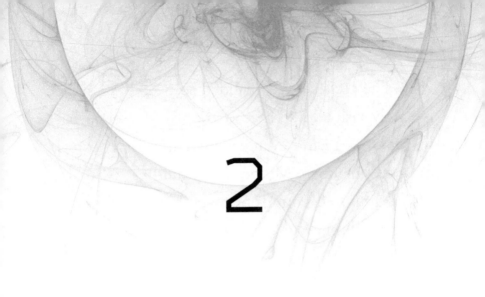

2

"**I**T'S NOT—"

"It is," I say.

Burnett shakes her head like a nervous twitch. Her gaze returns to her hands on the floor. "Not real," she says.

"Doctor," I say, as commandingly as I can. "This is happening . . . "

"Don't—don't believe him. No proof."

"They're dead. They're all dead." I feel my anger growing. "And you need to get outta my way. Right now."

"Here we are," Dad said as they pulled up to the curb of Andre's middle school this morning. Andre pulled at the heavy backpack crammed into the foot well in front of him. Dad craned his neck to look up through the windshield. "Looks like it might rain," he observed of the gray clouds looming overhead. Andre grunted when the bag finally came free and up to his lap.

"Hey," Dad said as Andre turned for the door handle. "How about a hug for the old man before you go?"

"How about not?" Andre replied.

"How about this?" Dad said, pressing the auto lock button just as Andre pulled the door handle.

"Dad! I need to go. It's gonna rain."

"Oh, I know, horrible father making his kid hug him in public where someone might see. C'mon," Dad put his arms out, "humiliation builds character."

Andre rolled his eyes.

Dad sat there, arms wide.

"Fine," said Andre, leaning in to tap Dad on one shoulder as Dad awkwardly grabbed him from across the gap in the seats and over the backpack slumping in Andre's lap.

"Not so bad, right?" Dad asked, moving away. "And the only ones who saw were those girls over there." Andre rolled his eyes again. Dad unlocked the doors. Andre muttered something, hefted his bag up, and exited the car, slamming the door behind him.

Dad watched as Andre swung the bag onto his back, whole body swaying with the effort. He remained at the curb. Other cars pulled over and away around him. Dad watched until Andre passed through the gate and into the playground/parking lot of the school.

There was a black sedan parked in front of the house when Dad returned. "He's early," he said to himself. Mr. Aukerman watered the grass outside of his house. He nodded as Dad drove by. Dad pulled into the garage out front; Mom's car was still unmoved from the previous day. He paused right outside the garage, looked up at the overcast sky, took a breath, and continued on.

The front door and window had already been repaired. Choi stood up from his seat at the dining room table as Dad entered. Mom remained in her seat across from him, her back to the door. The coffee table in front of the television was straightened up, and any marks on the carpet from the soldiers' boots had been cleaned. The house looked like nothing happened there. They weren't informed of any altercation during their conversation yesterday which resulted in their scheduled meeting today. That meeting was supposed to begin an hour later.

"Mr. Lewis," Choi said, placing his hand out to shake before Dad even stepped from the living room carpet to the dining room tile. "Sorry to start our meeting early but I was eager to—"

"They want to move us," Mom said, still seated, staring across the width of the table at the man in the black suit with the spiky hair and earpiece. "They're forcing us to give up everything, again."

Choi pulled his hand away and sat down, straighter than the back of his chair. Dad took the seat next to Mom and tapped for her hand under the table. He took it when she didn't respond.

"First," said Choi, "as I said before, I want to thank both of you for all the sacrifice and service you've given to this project and to your country over the years."

Mom scoffed. Dad squeezed her hand.

"Regardless of the exact outcome, you did an amazing job in a very difficult and volatile circumstance. You did everything we asked without flaw or complaint and we accept full responsibility for any adverse result. We understand that turning Odin over to our custody was a difficult decision, but it was also the right one."

Dad exhaled heavily. Mom glanced at him quickly, as though trying to see how he would react. It was her decision to call them in, not his, and not theirs.

"Where is he?" Dad asked.

"Last I heard was that Odin provided excellent information on how to track down Wendell. He was cooperating and proving a valuable asset to the team. You should be very proud."

"And how much of that are we expected to believe?" Mom asked.

Choi exhaled, took a second to gather himself. "He's safe," he said, "and we're doing what we can to keep him that way. It's to that end, in fact, that I'm here. I promised Odin I would do everything in my power to keep you safe as well."

"Here comes another line of bullshit," said Mom.

"It's unfortunate," Choi continued, "but it's obvious that this location is compromised. We don't yet know all the consequences from yesterday's emergency protocol but we—Dr. Burnett, me, others in the Project, even Director Braxton himself—all feel that it's too dangerous to leave your family in this situation any longer. Not only dangerous for you and your son but also for those agents who have been tasked with assuring your safety. Your presence also places them in danger."

Mom scoffed once more. Dad rubbed his fingers against hers. She loosed her hand from his. "We place them in danger," she said. "Them."

"Honey," Dad whispered.

"We lived with that . . . that thing in this house, with our son, for years," she flung her arms wildly, "and now *we* are a danger to *them*. Where were they when he suddenly reappeared in this house? When he was right where we're sitting now? *They* didn't do anything. *We* had to fend for ourselves."

Dad took a long breath. Choi remained completely still, rigid as a tombstone.

"You never told us just how dangerous he would become. You never told us that. Now, after years of having a ticking bomb in our house, you tell us that we need to give up even more? That our son, our real son, who's been nothing but harmless and nearly forgotten in all this, has to give up his entire life because your people feel, *feel*," she stretched out the word, "that we might place *them* in danger." She shakes her head. "No. No. We've already given you everything we have. We've been through enough and our son has been through enough."

"Mrs. Lewis, I understand—"

"You know how hard it's been to keep up this lie for so long? Especially," she chuckled madly, "when you're lying to something that can read your goddamn mind?" She laughs. "I mean, we've had to speak in code for the last twelve years."

Choi said nothing. He knew better.

"But I did it. We did it." She glanced over at Dad, his brow furrowed in surprise and concern. "We did it because it was our job. It was our service to our nation. For the good of the whole goddamn world, we gave up our lives and our son's life and our safety. We've lied to our son, to our friends, the few friends we've been allowed to have before it compromises our situation," she waved her hands in ridicule, "to everyone for so long that I don't even know what the truth is."

Dad placed his hand on the table, offering it to her. Choi didn't move except to breathe.

"Last week Andre asked me when Odin would be coming back. He asked me this, right over there," she flung an arm out to indicate the living room behind her, the room that she didn't know had been repaired within an hour after they left the house yesterday morning. "He said he missed him." Water builds at the corners of her eyes. "And instead of saying what I wanted to say, that I was glad he was gone, that I hoped we never seen him again, I had to tell him that I missed him too and that he would be back soon." She shook her head. "How can I expect my son to believe a word I've ever said to him when his entire life has been a lie?" She took a moment to calm and wipe at her eyes before folding her arms in front of her. "But that's not your concern is it? Never was."

Choi glanced over to Dad. Dad looked back, eyes narrowed. He wasn't upset for himself. Choi looked down at the table for a moment before meeting Mom's expectant stare.

"I honestly don't know how to answer that."

"No one can," she said.

"I can't imagine what it's been like for you." He placed his hands together in a prayer form, pointed in their direction. "Please, please, trust me when I say that we wouldn't ask you to sacrifice anything more unless it was absolutely necessary. This, relocating you to a new city, is absolutely necessary."

Mom thrust back hard against the seat. The legs scraped against the tile floor. Dad rubbed her shoulder.

"Could we at least allow Andre to finish out the school year here?" he asked. "He'll be starting high school after the next summer so it could be a fresh start for everyone. I think for everything we've done, we're at least owed that much."

"You are owed," Choi paused, "a lot. And we're willing to give you a lot. Not as much as you deserve but much more than we could—" he stopped. He stared out the front window at a white glow outside pouring into the house. Dad turned to see.

"Get under something," Choi said, pushing his chair back to stand up.

Mom turned.

"Get under some—"

"It's him isn't it?" Mom yelled.

The light grew brighter through the living room window.

Dad sprung up from the table and rushed to see what was happening. Choi reached for the phone in his pocket. Mom stood and spun to watch. "It's him! That monster!" yelled Mom.

Choi pressed one button and put the phone to the ear with the hearing aid in it. Dad shielded his eyes to look out the window. "It's everywhere," he said. Mom strained to see him in the light across the room. "Ben, Andre!" she yelled at him.

There was a loud crunch against the roof. A ceiling board over the dining room cracked. It swung down hard, smashing Choi across the head. Mom dropped to the floor and under the table. Choi fell on the ground in front of the chair. His open eyes stared directly at Mom. Blood rushed from the wound on his head and across his face. She screamed. The rest of the roof came down. Dad disappeared in the rubble and the light.

"That monster," Mom said in panic. "That fucking monster."

The table above her collapsed.

"Move!" I roar at Burnett.

She turns to stare at me. Her eyebrows are up.

Her eyes are huge and watery. Heavy rings sag beneath them. "Go!" I yell at her.

It doesn't matter what was said. Dad. Mom. Choi. I can't see any of them beyond that moment when the roof came down. They no longer exist.

I fix my feet to the ground and press my back flat against the wall. I squeeze every muscle in my arms and chest, those that actually respond. I brace myself.

Aida and I—Mom and I—were never that close. But she still treated me well. Must have been hard to hold those feelings in for so long.

Ben—Dad—was always a good guy. He believed in me. I could see it, even in the end.

Their choice or not, they sacrificed themselves. For me. For what I could do.

I see a blur as Wendell turns from the machine toward us. "What are you—?"

He took them away. From me. From this world.

Reclamation and protection have failed. There is only revenge left.

Burnett scrambles toward the computer room door. Pain surges through my chest. I push my left arm forward. The metal covering rips from the wall. It streaks across the room at Wendell in a silver flash. The metal piece angles off in front of him. It smashes into the back corner of the room. I try to move my right arm. Pain flares down my entire side. I swing the left around instead. I toss the second metal piece out. It hits something. Doesn't matter what. I steady myself on the ground with my feet solid below me. My right arm hangs like dead meat from my side.

Redness creeps into the ends of my vision, him standing in the middle. All I see is him, and how I'm going to rip him apart. There is only revenge.

3

"**S**O YOU ARE NOT COMPLETELY DISCONNECTED AFTER all." He says. "Good." He steps from the side of the machine to the front of it, blocking the open end of the metal tunnel.

I fling several large chunks of broken wall. They fly faster than I can see. They make impact in the air several feet in front of him. They burst into dust and gravel.

My right arm sways lifelessly. I fire more rubble at him, a handful of rocks with more force than a wrecking ball. They don't drop. He turns them away. They dent the walls and crack the glass blocking the computer station. Maybe I can catch

44

him off guard. I send a second handful immediately after. I hear pops and pings. "Ah!" he says. One rock sparks off a panel in the machine. He wipes at a thin line of blood forming on his forehead.

"You have always been a fool," he says.

I grit my teeth and growl at him.

He slams my back against the wall. The impact shakes my bones. It hurts badly. It's not nearly as bad as it could have been. Must be placing more of his attention on the field around him. How far does it extend?

Another metal arch flies toward me. I catch it in flight. It freezes in the air, caught between his push toward and my push away. Equal but opposite forces. He could crush me, like he did Delgado or . . . everyone.

"I wonder," he says, "if you are again part of the anomaly, does that mean I can finally kill you?"

I drop to the floor. My shoulder hits the ground hard. The piece crashes into the wall above me. Broken concrete bits rain down. The arm hurts so much it's almost numb until the slightest movement or pressure, then it fires pain through my entire right side from my neck to my leg.

As I stand, I catch Burnett pulling open the door to the computer room. I throw another mass of broken wall at Wendell to keep his attention on me. He knocks everything I throw aside, like he's swatting flies. I expected he would. In the corner of my eye is the rubble from the crashed elevator. Several thin metal pieces have broken off the gate. A foot-thick chunk of the elevator car floor has severed rebar sticking out. I toss it at him. He catches this too. It doesn't move. I keep it there, pressing it forward, wanting it to break through. I fling another piece of elevator floor. It too stops. I let those two masses drop and launch a third at the broad side of the machine, far behind where his shield should end.

The jagged slab of concrete stops short of the metallic covering. I keep it there, pushing it forward with as much focus as I can. It slides along a dome of energy covering Solar Flare's length. He's guarding the entire machine. I release and the mass's inertia carries it over. It crashes to the floor on the other side of the metal tunnel. It didn't drop like the bullets outside. There is still force behind it. Maybe he can still be overwhelmed.

I picture the entire pile of elevator rubble—the shattered floor with its exposed support beams, the twisted metal gate and its broken pieces, the interior walls with the panel of up and down buttons—as much matter as possible—flying off as one cluster of mass hitting along the side of the machine, plowing into and through his shield like a landslide taking down a house. The rubble smashes against his invisible wall. It breaks like a wave over a reef. I hear a few strips of fence penetrate through, a metal-on-metal sound scratching across the outer shell. I keep the pressure on, pushing the entire elevator toward the machine's finished rings. He doesn't even look. He keeps his eyes on me and his focus on the machine as he pictures it behind him. Or, maybe, he sees the machine through my eyes so I won't surprise him.

I glance to the computer station. Burnett sits at one of the terminals. She stabs blindly at the keys. I can see that she's managed to locate the shutdown folder, but can't do anything it with. She doesn't know the orders or pass codes nor where to find them.

I keep the pressure against Wendell's invisible shield. Sustaining force has always been harder than causing it. Maybe it's the same holding back sustained force compared to merely stopping a one-time burst.

There wouldn't be a flood protocol for shutdown this time, not in the desert. Looking into a technician has always worked for Wendell. I picture the room itself before the facility was secured for our arrival. There were eight people in that room making final adjustments to the program prior to initial testing, pointing out errors in the coding and—the glass cracks in front of Burnett.

The cracking stops before any single break reaches through the depth of the glass. The jagged lines remain, like lightning bolts splintering through the window.

"Why do you continue to protect her?" Wendell says.

I growl in response. I let the elevator rubble drop to the floor, again. It crashes like a ton of bricks.

I keep my eyes on him and hold one hand out as I shuffle to the front of the computer room. My right arm swings painfully at my side. He watches me. The length of the machine comes into view. Two invisible lines drawn in the sand. The machine behind his. Burnett and the computer station behind mine. We are exact parallels. In line. Separate.

"Why her of all people?" he asks. "The one who attempted to program you. Why does she deserve to live?"

"She's all that I have left," I say from between clenched jaws.

One line of blood is smeared on his forehead. Fresh blood no longer flows from the cut. He's holding that back too. "That is right," he says. "You could not save any of the others."

I again bare my teeth at him. It's barbaric, but feels natural.

"Not your family, your friends, not one of them."

My nostrils flare.

"You failed, Odin. Once again. You failed."

A roar bellows out from the middle of my chest. A feral cry shakes my entire body. I want the building to collapse on top of us. I want the walls to explode, like my old house did, the house where I grew up and where I learned everything that has made me who I am. I want to bury us both.

The lights overhead shatter. Their covers and thin supports snap. The glass falls to the floor, breaking over his field like waterfalls. The shards

jingle on impact. I don't try to move it. I focus
on creating a wall between him and me, the same
way he did holding the water back at Colton or
the bullets outside. I create a field of energy across
the full face of the room. Nothing gets through the
glass in front of the computer station.

He sneers, "Looks like we both have something
holding us back."

I hear the echo of my heart thumping. The fingers I can move squeeze the air in front of me. The
pulse in my right arm is like tiny needles running
through my veins.

"You know that even without the program, I
can still use this machine."

I let him talk. It means he has less focus to
defend or attack.

Burnett glances through the window at us.
Spider web cracks obscure her view, breaking
Wendell and I into fractured pieces of ourselves.
On the screen in front of her. unfamiliar folder
names branch from equally unfamiliar folders. She

pushes the papers around on the desk, trying to find anything about Solar Flare's shutdown procedure.

"Look at her," he says, "she is so lost."

Broken light bulbs and bits of shattered wall hover inches above the machine. I picture Solar Flare crushing in on itself the same way I pictured the elevator floor flying or the dead space in front of me. But nothing happens. His force is equal to mine. Newton's Third Law, applied in a way I doubt even he could have imagined.

"I know exactly what to do," he says, in the same calm voice I used to use when explaining answers to Brent when he took Algebra II last year. "Exactly how to make it work. I have done it before."

His eyes start to glow. The machine begins to hum.

"You can't," I grunt. "You wouldn't." I know he hates being told what to do. Especially when

I'm the one that tells him. It'll make him do the opposite.

"You still think that?"

Bits of glass fall onto the machine behind him, tapping on the metal shell. The light from his eyes reflects off the blood drop gathering on his forehead. He's placing his concentration elsewhere. Preparing something.

"Have I not proven my will?" he says.

I grind my teeth at him. Can't press too hard. Let him think this is his idea.

The front-most segment of the machine begins to turn. Other segments rumble into motion down the rest of the line. I listen for the sound of glass tapping or the broken concrete thumping against the outer shell. I tune in for those noises over the hum of the machine gradually growing louder as more of it spins. The effort of moving and sustaining each of these parts must be tremendous. Just keeping them all in mind at the same time, enough to control their rotation, is taking so much of his focus. It's making his guard wane. He must know this. I have to make my move before he can adjust. An unused piece of Solar Flare's shell remains lodged in the wall where I dropped to the floor beneath it. If he can generate enough power to dig its ends into solid concrete, then I can generate enough to get it out. I lock my eyes on his. I have to reveal nothing. I listen as the machine begins to speed up. Light starts to appear between the different segments and pours from the front and rear openings in the tunnel. Now.

The metal arch rips from the wall. Wendell turns. The round side of the shell rockets into him. It carries into the first machine segment. The piece smashes two feet into one side. The whole ring lifts slightly at impact. It drops back into place. The arch wedges between ring and platform. Sparks fly. The machine continues trying to spin with the metal arch holding it back, like a stick stuck into bike spokes, scraping and ripping through the front rim of the first ring.

He rises quickly from the floor. Must've shielded himself from full impact. I fling bits of rubble at him. They burst into nothing. The machine stops spinning. The hum, the light, the vibration, all disappear. His eyes glow an intense white. They crackle. I feel them burning the air between us. I focus on the blank space in front of me and the window and wall extending on either side. I picture a thick layer of nothing three feet from the end of my outstretched arm. It's not a solid wall. It's an empty one. A gap in the world where nothing can exist. Not even atoms exist there. It's an unbreakable blank.

Everything near him begins to rise. Every shard of shattered glass, every chunk of broken concrete, every rock and pebble and broken metal strip and heavy slab, they all rise from around and behind him. It's like the fur standing on the back of an enraged animal.

Don't try to stop every individual object. That's not what he does. Focus on the place in front of the objects. I don't have to keep the objects in mind to stop them. I can't. But I can keep one place in my head. One place big and solid enough to hold everything else out.

The glass flies. The rocks and stones. Chunks of wall. Metal sheets. The elevator gate, and floor, and interior with the panel of up and down buttons. They thump on the wall of emptiness in front of me. I feel the force behind it. The pressure builds. There's a pinch in my head. I hold these objects back in the air as he pushes them forward, it's like trying to bench press several times my weight, one handed. Won't be long until the force is too much.

I hear a pop. A quiet one. Outside. Glass and rocks fall from out of Wendell's control. His focus is decreasing. An explosion shakes the room. Debris drops or launches outward. Another pop. Light bangs and taps follow. More objects fall from Wendell's control. A second explosion cracks the wall above the main entrance. Wendell drops everything. There's a scream from outside as something arcs toward the buildings. A hole blasts through the upper wall.

The force knocks me sideways. I hit the ground hard.

4

ANDRE LEANED FORWARD SLIGHTLY TO ACCOMMODATE the weight of his backpack, the way a mountain climber does while ascending a tremendous slope. He placed his hands under the straps, again cutting a little of the pressure on his shoulders. We once weighed his bag when it was fully loaded with seven classes worth of textbooks, and it was also just over twenty pounds, or nine kilograms, about the same as mine. At fifty-six inches in height, although he's taller now, that's just over one hundred twenty-five joules of potential energy on a thirteen-year-old boy. He kept his head angled down as he crossed over the track of the sliding gate onto his middle school's campus.

Several of the boys, mostly seventh and eighth graders, tossed a couple of basketballs at the two hoops set up in the paved central area which served as a parking lot during open house nights and parent-teacher conferences. The classrooms rimmed around. Administration at the front had the only exit once the gate was closed. A few bare trees dotted the open spaces between the classes and small patches of grass gathered around their roots with brown spots from where the leaves fell and remained to die. The layout naturally allowed students to mingle in the center while moving between classes in the morning, at lunch, or passing each other on their way to and from different periods. Sometimes, during the cold months, it made the simplest transition between neighboring rooms a five-minute process of adding and removing layers of outerwear, which some students used to delay classes.

Andre walked on, hunched over as he was, toward his homeroom near the back left corner. He stepped up the stairs to peek inside. He saw a few backpacks at the desks but no one was there. He left his bag on the seat of his desk along the rear wall and walked back outside. He sat down on the second lowest stair just off the path between doors. His feet were planted on the asphalt that the other kids played on.

He didn't like the clouds. He told me once that they made it feel like the day never started. Gray skies, like those that usually mean rain, made him think of the morning before the real day begins, when there is still the entire day ahead, or late afternoon, when the day is over and it's time to go home. He said it's like you're waiting all day. Maybe that's how he felt sitting on the stairs in front of his classroom. Most of the girls in his grade gathered at the benches lining the school's concrete playground, texting back and forth while sitting next to each other. Some of his friends clanked a basketball off the eight-foot rim and took turns trying to see who could come closest to touching the hoop. It was only the tall kids, Cameron and Russell, who could get close, and even they were several inches off. Cameron always stuck his tongue out when he jumped. He said it was to make him jump like Jordan. Alvin joked that one day he'd land and bite his tongue off.

Alvin didn't like Cameron, from that time when they'd first started at this school when Cameron shoved him against the wall and kept him there by locking his arms against Alvin's shoulders. For no reason, Alvin would complain, no reason at all. Cameron said he was just playing, but he never apologized. Cameron was the tallest kid in the class though, so most of the other boys liked him, the ones who played basketball in the morning at least.

"Good morning, Andre," said Andre's social studies and homeroom teacher, Mrs. Moreland, as she approached the bottom of the short staircase into the room. Theirs was one of only four buildings that had stairs. These classrooms were added after severe rain flooded the original campus years ago.

Her heels tapped twice with each step. She wore a black skirt, a red top that showed off surprisingly fit arms, and carried a laptop bag she used for her papers and books. She was in her thirties and had green eyes. His friend, Greg, liked to tell the story about the time he had to stay back from the end-of-the-year field trip in sixth grade and was told to study quietly at his desk while Mrs. Moreland corrected homework. She'd just started at the school that year so she wasn't yet as hated as the other teachers. He spent the entire day staring down her shirt. The first time he told the story, it was her black bra strap that was visible. By the eighth time the bra was gone and her tits practically burst through her top.

"Is everything all right?" Andre heard, following a pair of double taps at the top of the stairs, after she had dropped her bag and stepped outside.

"Fine," he said, looking up at Mrs. Moreland behind him.

"Are you sure?" she said, making a slight pout. "You have the whole day to sit. Why not play with the others?"

He shook his head.

"Something wrong?" Moreland asked.

He shook his head again.

Moreland carefully descended one stair, stepped to the side of the staircase, out of the way, and spun around before sitting. She leaned forward and crossed her legs, her toes pointing toward the ball court. "C'mon," she said, "talk to me."

"It's just weird," he said, looking down at his shoes.

"What's weird?"

"Everything."

"Yeah," she said, "the world's weird. Not much we can do about that." She smiled wryly. Andre didn't see it. "Can you be a bit more specific?"

He looked around for a moment. The other

kids seemed occupied by other things. No one else was near or approaching. "It's almost Christmas break and my brother isn't around. He's always around for Christmas."

"Where is he?"

"College. Mom and Dad said it's this special program that started early, so he had to just leave a few months ago."

"That's good. I'm sure he'll be home soon."

"But I haven't talked to him since he left. Mom and Dad don't even talk about him anymore."

"Hmmm," she said, nodding. Andre didn't see that either. He stared at his shoes, glancing up once as one of his classmates ascended the stairs into the room.

"It's like there's something going on, but like they don't want to talk about it. They used to talk about him, but then they stopped."

"Have you asked?" She motioned her head around as though angling to get into his line of sight. "If it's bothering you, I'm sure they'd tell."

"No," he shook his head. "I think it would just cause trouble. My parents don't really like when we ask questions. Dad says there's a reason people keep certain things secret."

"Hmmm," she said again. "You know what, Andre?"

He looked up finally, eyes landing directly on her chest. He looked down again quickly, and then up to her eyes.

"That *is* weird," she said nodding. "But maybe they're just trying to make things less weird. The first holiday away is always going to be strange. There's still a couple of weeks left before the break begins. I'm sure your brother will be back before then."

Andre looked away blankly.

"No reason for him not to be?" Mrs. Moreland asked.

"I guess not."

The other students rushed down the stairs to join the last minute of the basketball game.

"Maybe they're just keeping it a secret so it can be this big surprise when he comes back. That would be pretty fun, right?"

"I guess so."

"You know, I think you should be more confident about that. No more guessing. That would be pretty fun, right?"

He looked at her and nodded.

"Let's hear it."

He rolled his eyes. "That would be pretty fun."

"Yeah," she said, "that's the spirit." Sarcasm dripped from her words.

He nodded again, but not confidently.

"Feel a little less weird no—"

Movement caught their attention, shadows contracting into single spots as the sky lit up brightly. The clouds became invisible against the light behind it. Andre looked over to Mrs. Moreland, her neck craned directly up so that the bones in her neck formed a strong V, like an arrow pointing to the hint of cleavage peeking from the top of her shirt. The light grew. All colors diluted. Everything uncovered was drowned by light. There were shadows and nothing else.

"What's happening?" Andre said.

"Don't know," answered Mrs. Moreland. She stood up to stare at the sky.

"Is it a bomb?"

Mrs. Moreland muttered, "What the f—"

The top of the room smashed down. Andre pulled his feet up to lie on the step. The basketball hoops crumbled. The teachers yelled for the kids to get under something. The kids ran around screaming. Some crammed under the benches. Andre rolled down the stairs to the ground. Mrs. Moreland tapped her way down behind him. Andre lay flat. His feet twitched nervously. Children screamed. He couldn't see them.

He looked around and saw light. No more clouds. No sky. No trees. No buildings. Mrs. Moreland slipped on the last stair. She fell back onto the steps. Her heel kicked Andre in the leg.

She tried to stand. The light pressed downward. Andre covered the back of his head with his hands. He buried his face in the asphalt. Mrs. Moreland screamed. Her head disappeared. Blood splattered Andre's arm. Mrs. Moreland stopped moving. Andre squeezed his eyes tightly. The light burned through.

My eyes shoot open as though I'm coming up from a bad dream. I wish I were. Where is the bastard?

I jump to my feet before the pain catches up. A stabbing sensation runs from the fingers in my right hand to my shoulder. The cuts on my forearms sting but don't bleed too badly, not like what Wendell did to everyone else, and nothing compared to what I'll do to him when I can.

A dull light shines through a hole blown in the wall above the main entrance to the building. The concussion must've knocked me down. Bits of rubble explode outward, from the building itself and from the large piles pulled into a protective shell against the perimeter. Large slabs and small rocks litter the floor. One mass of rock crashed down only a few feet from where I'd been tossed. Another slammed into Solar Flare, partially caving in the division between two of the sections. Still another large rock dropped where Wendell had been standing.

He's outside, in the hazy light of the overcast desert morning, hovering off the ground, over the road leading through the destroyed buildings gridded around this one. His eyes glow pure white, crackling, the empty space almost rippling around him. He charges forward, into a gathered throng of military vehicles, tanks, Humvees, troop transports. He tosses them aside as he progresses through. His palms turn up. The vehicles part from around him. This is him, unleashed, without the building or the machine to protect.

My first instinct is to chase him down, pound

his head into the road until his skull is a puddle of goo. Then my eyes catch on the shattered glass and piles of debris where Wendell dropped them. Solar Flare has one dented segment in front from where I slammed part of its unattached shell, and two other sections almost complete crushed under a large piece of wall. Delgado's body lies half-buried in the rubble. Then I remember what I have to do first, before ripping Wendell's head from his shoulders.

Large cracks stretch across the glass in front of the computer station. Lines splinter from several points of impact, but nothing seems to have broken through. Strong glass was used in case Solar Flare were to rupture during testing.

I turn the wheel handle on the door with the one hand I can actually use. It's nice to feel the cold metal and the tension in every pull. I yank the door open and walk in.

"Dr. Burnett?" I say, not seeing her anywhere.

I move around the row of computers. Burnett

flinches away before seeing me. She breathes out and leans back in relief. She climbs into the chair behind a computer. She doesn't look injured. "He's gone," I say. "Let's get rid of this thing."

I picture this room before the complex was evacuated. Technicians and engineers occupied the same space in a different time. I hold the word "emergency" while tracing through the last day.

"We can't," Burnett says. She looks up at me with the same placid expression she used to have when I would tell her about what I had for breakfast before one of my sessions in her office.

"He'll be back soon." I say, careful not to gesture too much, "I can find the emergency protocol and we can stop him from using it."

"Doesn't matter," she says. "The technology exists."

"We can at least destroy this machine," I say, trying my best not to yell at her. "It needs to be destroyed. Completely."

"Don't," she's slouched slightly, almost relaxed,

"this machine, this one," she points vaguely in the direction of the glass between this room and the wreckage in the other, "could be our last chance."

"What about their chances? The entire city, Doctor!" I feel myself growing angrier. "You didn't see it! Everyone I know died in the same instant. Screaming and panicked and saying it was my fault."

She looks as though she's about the cry.

"They died terrified." My lip quivers. I probably look like I'm about to cry too. "The least I can do is destroyed the thing that killed them."

"It wasn't the machine, Odin." Her eyebrows are raised in the middle, putting creases in her brow like umbrellas. "The technology has no control over how it's used. Just as you have no control over how you were used."

I shake my head. I'm somewhere between bawling and fuming.

"There's still a chance," she says, looking at the computer. The "Data" folder is opened to a long stream of subfolders. "We can salvage this. The program can still work."

I approach along the row next to her. "Doctor—"

"If it doesn't, then it means everything we've done—everything you've been through—is wasted." She turns to me now, eyes wet and shining, "We can't let that happen. Not now. Not when we've already lost so much."

"You didn't see what happened—"

"The machine has no agenda or desires. It's science; it has no point of view except what we give it. If we want to make it destructive, then it is destructive, but now, after what happened—"

"You don't know," I say.

"The destruction could be so much that it actually deters its use, like the A-bomb. They were used once and never again. New weapons were made but we knew better than to use them. We saw their destruction. It's a power source but not a weapon. Not anymore."

I shake my head. I should use this time to tear the machine apart myself.

"Nuclear power might be dangerous, but not this. It's safe, Odin. It's safe and it can save."

She didn't see it, the buildings reduced to rocks and ash, people crushed into puddles of powdered bones and blood, the roof beam cracking Choi's skull. Dad disappearing into the falling rubble. Mom using her last breath to damn me. My little brother, screw biology, pressing his face into jagged rocks to escape the force that crushed his entire school. It must have crushed my school too. Evelyn . . . I don't even want to . . .

I hear a crash against the building. Something heavy was tossed into the rubble still piled outside. I'll see what happened later. "We can't." I say. "It's too much to keep."

"Odin, I understand how you must feel," she says.

"You don't!" I snap at her. The glass window begins to crack.

"This data," she says, gripping onto the keyboard as though it were precious to her, "this science. It's all I have left. Without it . . . " she stares into the computer screen. "Without it, we really have lost everything."

She had to give up both her practice and her teaching position to join the DRDI. She told her husband it was for another opportunity, a position with a neuro-pharmaceutical lab researching causes and preventative steps against Alzheimer's. She picked that condition in particular knowing that her husband's biggest fear was spending his final years as unaware of his surroundings as his own mother did. Her husband had to stay behind to sell the house they spent years saving for. By the time he finally arrived in Washington to be with her, she was already so ingrained with Project Solar Flare, with me, that when she said she needed to relocate again, he refused. She never told me that she left her husband for this project. For me. She didn't have to be coerced or conditioned into being a part the experiment. She decided to give everything she had to it. If I am a victim, then she is a sacrifice.

She begs me from behind the computer.

"Stay safe," I say. "Try to contract Braxton or someone."

She nods. "Thank you," she says.

Another crash outside. Rocks fall.

I rush out the door into the computer station. I make sure to crank the handle as far as possible, wincing as the shaking effort sends a shock of pain through my entire hanging arm. I stretch my left arm across to squeeze my right arm in as I step over the uneven rocks and slabs and shattered glass and metal strips that form a solid line where I repelled Wendell's last attack.

The hole in the wall begins about thirty feet up and extends another six, a jagged scalene triangle blasted through and looking out onto the gray sky. There's still a slight haze of dust floating around the hole, diffusing the little bit of light that manages to escape through the clouds. A couple of bright slivers shine around the rim of a silvery gray cloud. I feel a momentary sting looking at them, like the wind blowing through the leaves in the backyard.

Two huge gaps remain in the gate where Wendell had me pinned. They blend with the rubble fallen from the hole blasted just a couple of feet from where I had been. Good thing I moved before then. A few blood drops remain visible while fresh debris covers the rest. Looks like the cuts have stopped bleeding. Might start again once I get out there and my heart rate increases. I could hold it back like Wendell did, but I should keep my attention on him. If I make him bleed enough he could become so focused on covering the wounds that he can't do anything else. Death by a thousand cuts.

Delgado's body has been tossed to the side of the building and now lies crushed under a slab like the Wicked Witch of the East. Solar Flare is busted in the front and the middle. The unused piece crammed between the first segment and the stand, pushing the staircase slightly off-center. Inside the tunnel I can see where the big chunk of wall has broken through between two segments. At least it isn't usable.

I lift myself up toward the hole in the wall. I'm actually flying. Makes sense but doing it now feels . . . like something special. I could go anywhere I want. Except . . . Another crash from outside. Wish I had the chance to enjoy this. Maybe afterwards. Maybe there will be time then.

A pair of Humvees lay at the foot of the rubble wall. Both vehicles folded in half. A third sits several dozen feet short of the rubble. Broken but not bent. A clear path is cut from the sealed entrance of the central building toward the front gate of the complex. The surrounding buildings, maybe three stories tall yesterday, are hollowed husks. Their contents have spilled out like intestines. Computer monitors, tables, desk chairs, there's even half a sink and a toilet with the seat ripped off mixed in the rest of the miscellaneous debris. Bodies are buried under the rubble. Several vehicles lie toppled on their sides. Smoke rises from a few. I can't tell which bodies are from this latest group and which were from the first. They're all the same now.

At the far end of the road through the facility, out near the opened gate and between a pair of torn-down guard towers, a scrawny figure lifts a tank straight up off the ground. The tank smashes in the middle, as though belted very tightly. There's the faint sound of metal shredding. The tank falls with a muted thud.

I see his glowing eyes from here as he turns. I wonder if my eyes glow too. I hope they do. I hope he feels them burning. No need to hold back now. Revenge. It's all I have left.

5

A STANDING COUNTER OF WORKSTATIONS DIVIDED THE room in half, with a gap in the middle to allow traffic through. Each of the twelve stations, arranged three by two on both sides of the room, had its own electric outlet, a sink with a tall, bending faucet, and enough space for whatever laboratory experiment was happening during that class. Bunsen burners and rolled-up rubber tubes were clustered between the last two stations on each side. The blackboards of both classrooms faced each other. Neat rows and columns of empty desks filled one room while several on the other side were pushed apart to form a circle so the students in them could talk. Kevin sat in one of the chairs. A female student sat against the attached desk in front of him.

His nose was straighter than before, a solid line from the top to the tip. His jaw, previously long and thin, seemed to have a little extra width to it. His mother suggested that change as Kevin was preparing for surgery to fix a loud clicking that happened every time he moved his mouth in the month following our fight. She said if they were going to have it fixed, why not also have it improved? He frowned, as much as he was able. She shrugged and said it was no secret that he had a bit of a horse face, but it was nothing that couldn't be corrected.

He started at his new school before the swelling had completely gone down. He told them it was from fighting off a group of kids with knives that jumped him outside his old school one day. That's why he needed surgery and why his parents decided to send him to St. Ambrose, a private school located right outside of where the down-town buildings grew tall. He said his parents were afraid that he be a target on account of jealousy.

The straight rim of his hat rose high in the air, like a sideways and slightly crooked fin near the top of his head. He wore a white shirt with long sleeves and a collar opened up just enough to show a gold necklace. On the back of his seat was a thick coat with a fur collar.

The girl half sitting on the front of his desk wore big red sunglasses, a white, collared shirt with no sleeves and a plaid gray-on-black skirt with striped black and red tights down to red shoes. Her top three buttons were open. A gold crucifix dangled in the shadow of her pushed-up cleavage. Kevin kept his hand on her right hip. The others in the room, six boys and two girls including Kevin and his hood ornament, spoke loudly and laughed louder.

There were no knives involved the first time he told the story of being jumped, over a Facebook message to Joseph, a guy we both knew from grade school and who had moved to Virginia right after we finished fifth grade. He was walking to his car after school when three guys—they looked like seniors from some other school, he wrote—approached from another car. They asked if that was his car and said it was nice and asked him how much money he had on him right then. He wouldn't say. He wrote that they said they'd count it themselves. That's when the first punch came, right to the jaw. He felt it crack but continued the fight. Three of them and him, throwing blows. They almost had him on the ground when he grabbed one of them and tossed him over his shoulder, like a fucking ninja, he wrote. The other two were so scared that they stopped fighting and moved away. He got in his car and stared at them until they left. He said he was ready to run them down if he had to. It was only after he got home that he noticed how badly they had beaten him.

Must've been adrenaline or something, didn't even feel it before.

"Holy shit!" Joseph replied. "You all right now?"

"Fine, had to get my nose fixed and jaw wired for a little while but I'm all right. Nothing big."

It was when telling the story in person that he added the knife, but other than that, it was pretty much the same. He also removed all his old photos from his Facebook account and unfriended and blocked everyone from our old school. He saw a few of them while getting lunch a while ago, Derek, Calvin, a couple other baseball guys, but pretended he didn't know them. He looked different enough that they weren't sure. He never mentioned me or any of the others. It was a completely different life, one that never actually existed.

He kept his hand firmly on his girlfriend's hip as she balanced with her ass pushed up at the end of the desk. "I swear," she said, "the way Mrs. McConnell acts, it's like her and Mr. McConnell haven't fucked in, like, forever."

A couple of the others laugh. Kevin does too, even though he hadn't either. Not all the way. Not with anyone.

"She's all, like, 'Whitney, you need to apply yourself more.' I'm like for what? I didn't even wanna take fucking French. I'm only in the class because my dad fucking made me take it because his, like, grandparents or whatever spoke French and now I have to."

"You totally didn't say that," the other girl replied.

"Of course not, but I wanted to. So I was like, 'Yes, Mrs. McConnell.'" She fluttered her eyes sweetly. "Bitch."

Kevin smiled at that. His left hand hung off the chair while the fingers of his right spread and curved over the pleats of her skirt. He leaned back smirking like the kingpin of some white-collar crime family.

"Spanish is so much better," one of the other students said, a guy with a mustache that looked like a thin layer of dirt across his upper lip. "Mrs. Ramirez," he rolled both the R's in her name, "doesn't give a shit what we do as long as we roll our R's," he rolled them again, "in the right places."

Whitney made a gurgling sound. "See, I can't even do that," she said.

"I'm sorry," the boy said.

"Why?"

"I meant that I'm sorry for your boyfriend."

The others laughed.

"She's great at other things with her mouth," Kevin said with a cocky grin. "Not that you'll ever know."

"That's fucking right," Whitney snapped.

Kevin acted like the story of the three guys with the knife in the parking lot was this deep, dark secret that no one should ever hear. Every time he told it was with this hushed tone, as though it was painful to remember. One month into the school year, he'd shared it with half the senior class. The details changed, but the story was always preceded by the same reluctant, confessional sigh. Two months into the year and his story spread to the rest of the class. A few days later it moved down to the juniors through Whitney when he was trying to impress her so she'd go out with him. It eventually got down to the freshmen, who didn't know who Kevin was when he'd walk by until one of them would whisper, "That's the guy who got jumped by three guys with knives."

"Oh yeah?"

"Yeah, I heard he was like a two-time state jiu-jitsu champion."

"For real?"

"Yeah, and the city is named after his grandfather or something."

"Really?"

"I dunno but that's what I heard." New school, same old stories.

A man in glasses and a long overcoat walked in. Kevin pulled his hand away as Whitney bolted up from the chair. "Good morning," the man said, not looking at them. They all went still and quiet. The teacher placed a messenger bag on the desk and removed a thick binder from it. Kevin looked at everyone else and made a jerk-off motion. The others tried not to laugh. The teacher consulted the binder to draw chemical bonds on the board. He stopped to look up at the clock. "Almost time to start," he said, "I trust you are all in the right class." He glanced back at them. "Ms. Evans, Mr. James, Ms. Hall."

The group shifted around, lifting their bags and straightening the desks. Whitney took her bag and coat from the desk next the one she'd occupied with Kevin. Kevin stood up after her.

"Mr. Clark," the teacher said, "You are in the right class, but in the wrong fashion."

"I know," Kevin replied, ripping his hat off and tossing it into the seat. "Don't need to remind me, shithead," he muttered as he exited the room behind Whitney and the rest of the group.

Outside, Kevin looked around to see other

students making their way to class. Hundreds of white shirts moved across the path around them and in the school courtyard below. He reached out to smack Whitney's butt.

"Hey," she said, turning and smiling. "Not here. Or," she said, looking at the other students shambling by, "not right now."

"Maybe after sch—"

Every student froze to stare as the sky lit up above them. Kevin put his hand over his face and squinted into the burning white sky. The school building shook. The students on the third floor path started screaming. Their heavy footsteps sounded like an elephant stampede. Kevin and Whitney stared up at the dingy floor above them. He put his hand on her back. Whitney grabbed the cross between her tits. They jumped as a crack split the floor above them. "Oh Jesus," Whitney whispered. More cracks appeared. The floor above collapsed. Kevin pulled Whitney in with both arms. He fell on top of her. The floor fell on top of them.

It feels like seconds stretch into minutes, yet only enough time to move through instinct. Is that the way Kevin felt as the unknown light came crashing down? His instinct was to try to save his girlfriend. I tried saving all of them. Neither of us succeeded. We tried. Now, I pick up the pieces.

Wendell turns to see me too late. I am a bullet. I am a cannonball. I am a comet streaking across the open expanse at a speed greater than human sight.

There's an overturned personnel carrier on the side of the road. I fling it at him as I come to a halt. I picture my momentum shooting it forward. The sudden stop causes a surge of pain down my arm. I don't wince. I growl. The carrier flies toward him. Looks like he's hit. The carrier stops. It floats for a moment. It comes flying back.

I feel the carrier bounce off the empty air in front of me, a trick I learned from him. I saw him use it in Colton, imagined in Krieger, and watched in the building at the end of the road behind me. He tosses the crumbled tank. I turn it away like I'm smacking a crumpled wad of paper. He throws a piece of fallen tower wall. I spot a crack in the side. I split the wall in half before it reaches me. I direct a broken piece of road at him. It stops in the distance between us.

He looks almost gray in the dim light, and sick and painfully thin. He's a stick figure dressed in old drapes. I can't picture a single instance of him eating the whole time I was gone and after that. He could be feeding off the energy in his head. The brain commands the body to respond. He must be using the conduit in his mind to keep moving, shocking it like a defibrillator on a stopped heart.

I step forward. I continue pressing the hunk of asphalt. Thirty feet and infinite worlds separate us. A network of visible veins course through his neck and arms so pronounced that they cast their own shadows. The flakes of dead skin remain around his nose and forehead. The blood doesn't drip from his cut anymore. I wonder if it moves at all.

"Monster!" I yell at him, pressing forward.

He shakes his head. "People only say that of something they cannot control."

I feel the center of my brain pulsing. My whole body tingles. I am not holding a fork in the wall socket. I am the socket. I am the current and the electric plant. I am the energy that powers the world. So is he. And he knows it even better than I do.

"I keep trying to tell you, Odin, this is not your world." I see every muscle in his face tense as he speaks. "This is my world." He shifts sideways. I let the rubble between us fly off. He floats in a big arc circling me. Fallen bodies push aside as he passes, as though clearing a path through a crowded sidewalk. "This world I created long ago," he says. "It is beyond saving."

"You're right," I say, "everything I wanted to save is gone."

"You have no idea."

A trio of dead soldiers shoot toward me. I push them aside. I see one streak toward a stone barricade. I turn before it hits. A wet sound follows.

"I don't care," I say. "All I have left is punishing you. Making you pay for their lives in this world."

His arc continues until he's between me and the Solar Flare building.

"In this world," he says. "Only this world. They still live. You could see them. You could see anyone you want billions of times over." The glow in his sunken eyes makes him look like Death itself. "I could send you back there. You know you can do anything you want. Give this world to me and I will give you all the others."

He drifts backwards slowly. A few buildings remain mostly intact on the ends of the road around him. I ready for him to charge toward Solar Flare. I picture the loose materials around me rising. Pieces of road, building scrap, sandbags, a detached fender, float in stationary orbit. It's my own debris field.

"What do you hope to do here, Odin? You are too late. The change has already taken place."

I fire every piece of debris I have at him. I let him turn them away.

The buildings on either side of him tremble. Their foundations pull from the ground. I picture them coming together, like a pair of hands on a mosquito. They're a blur as they fly. They collide with him. Concrete and metal explodes.

A gray haze rises from the impact. Paths of wreckage lead from the sides of the road to the crash site. Two gaping holes cut into the row of short buildings. A few others remain intact. I know he's in there. I can imagine him through the dust.

The dust continues to rise from the flat land that used to be my city. Police and military personnel have closed off all the roads that lead to the area. There are traffic stops to re-route cars several miles away. The initial crowd remains, growing in the minutes since I last saw it, but not by much. Boats have strung buoys across the lake. Helicopters enforce a no-fly order against news choppers trying to film anything that may peek through the dust cloud.

Under that cloud of ash and death is the house where I grew up. It's now a burial site, the neighborhood where a team of Homeland Security agents watched in case my parents needed their help to control me. I doubt thirty seconds was enough warning to get out of town. There's my brother's school, Kevin's new school, my old school with the library where Evelyn told me about how she wished she could actually *be* Bianca instead of acting like her, the lunch room where Brent and David the traitor debated headshots, and the office where my suspicions were confirmed as Choi first mentioned the custody that led to the entire city being destroyed. Suspicions were put into my head by Wendell, the butterfly with the catastrophic wings.

The only motion in the dust is that of the emergency workers in the hazmat suits and gas masks. They stagger through the loose remains flattened into the earth. They carry flashlights to see through the thick fog, but can't see more than a few feet ahead. They trip over the buildings smashed downward. The road is more cracked than whole. The bones of the people are more gas than solid, the bodies more liquid than . . . people.

I can hear a few of the workers talking to each other over Walkie Talkies and phones wired into their hazmat suits. They can't tell where to start searching for answers. They can't even tell what streets they're on, or if they are on a street. They don't know what could have caused such devastation other than nothing they could ever imagine. They haven't found any survivors and don't expect to, not in destruction as thorough as this, where even the pipes below the streets are exposed and broken. One of them calls it the biggest mass grave in history, except that very little of it is buried. It's all right on the surface.

The main highway into downtown is still swarmed with people. Many of them are reporters standing in front of big cameras, beaming images of police in riot gear with shotguns for bean-bags and tear gas grenades, trying to hold back the members of the screaming crowd who aren't reporters. An officer with a bullhorn behind a bar-ricade of armored police vehicles yells for everyone to disperse. "For your own safety disperse, please disperse!"

Someone in the crowd demands to know what they're hiding. Another yells that the people have a right to know if they're under attack. Still another shouts that terrorists must have set off a bomb in the city. The bullhorn officer says to remain calm, please remain calm. Someone in the crowd carries a handwritten sign declaring that the end of days is coming and demands that everyone else repent. He parades his message behind a on-camera news reporter urging viewers to remain patient, that they will deliver any new information as soon as they have it. Another reporter is struck silent. He nearly weeps on camera as he relates stories trickling in of people around the country trying to call their loved ones in the city or walking through the crowd with pictures of the person they'd lost. One man in a bomber jacket screams into a microphone about foreign invaders and jihadists and taking up arms against the coming assault on freedom.

An anchor on a different television channel sits behind his desk in New York and rattles on about how the entire scene is faked by the government to make the nation scared and docile. He cries, "False flag," and commands that anyone on the scene watch for black helicopters and film anyone trying to come through the barricades, especially if they're in uniform. The screen behind him mixes old images of black-booted law enforcement marching through urban areas with new footage of my destroyed city. Still another reporter in a studio only a few floors away from the other begs forgiveness for whatever crimes would bring such divine punishment upon humanity. She shouts and prays and begs for all others to do the same. Meanwhile, everything they know about my city—and everything I know of my world—is dust.

I hear a creak from between the conjoined buildings ahead. A rumble grows from the center out. Rocks shake loose. Metal shards rattle. I take a long breath to steady myself. A single pop pushes both structures aside. The concave walls around him fit the shape of his little bubble. He stands there, arms out at each side as if parting the seas, untouched.

"What do you think you can do?" he says.

I scowl in response.

"Even if you somehow win, whatever that means, you will never be able to live in this world. Not after all this." He gestures to the destruction around us, as if it were a reasonable sample of everything he's done. "There are already discussions happening about how to deal with us."

An image jumps into my mind of Braxton standing against a wood-paneled wall in a crowded room. People in suits and military uniforms are gathered around a long table. A dozen sit, all the others stand, packed so tightly there's barely room to pass. High on each wall are monitors showing a live feed of Wendell and me standing near the front gate of the destroyed facility. The colors are almost completely washed out.

"There is no escape for you," he says. "There never was."

I exhale loudly through my nose, a bull ready to charge.

"I tried to help you make this the one among infinite worlds not ruled by chaos. One in which no one had to suffer without reason, even if it was manufactured."

"This *is* chaos. This *is* suffering without reason."

He shakes his head as though disappointed. "I have done everything possible to make you understand, Odin. I even led you to a place where you could see the ways of nature for yourself. A place where the scope of time is not so limited as it is here."

My right arm hangs, throbbing uselessly.

"Yet you do not even try to see anything outside of yourself."

I close my left fist so tight I feel my pulse beating along every finger.

"Such potential. Such waste."

His pupils go completely white while the whites of his eyes go dark.

"I have no need of such waste."

He seems to go still for a moment. A distant look appears on his face. It's the same look I have when watching something else. He blinks out of it. "Fools," I barely hear him say. He swings one scrawny arm. One of the collapsed buildings flies toward me. I push myself away, dodging it in a blink. The second building follows. Another dodge. My movement is almost like teleporting. I feel the motion in my arm. I try to ignore it, outwardly at least.

There's a crack in the road between us. It's small and shallow, but I can see it there. I picture it in my head breaking across the entire street. I swing my arm at the seam in the asphalt. Every layer of the road splits down to the rock below, exactly as I imagined. I lift the road up. It's one page of a huge textbook. Wendell disappears from my view. I push the strip of road up until it breaks. I throw it like a wall. Wendell shoots upward to avoid it. The block of road falls. I follow him into the air.

The emptiness feels solid under my feet. He moves upright into the overcast sky. I do the same in pursuit. He almost blends into the mass of gray clouds that have gathered over the complex. Only his glowing eyes mark his location. Odd for the desert to have such heavy storm clouds. Another anomaly here. The complex below is monochromatic gray as well. The large length of asphalt I ripped from the road, the buildings reduced to rock piles, the vehicles crushed into scrap metal, and the bodies, mangled but still identifiable, all blend into one mass of destruction.

I see Braxton again. The monitors along the upper walls in that room show almost the same exact picture. The camera zooms out slowly. The flat desert stretches into the distance. Another monitor shows a different angle of the same scene. At least two drones must be nearby. Unarmed, I hope.

Wendell continues upward. His glowing eyes leave a trail behind him. I follow it. He flies around as though searching for something in the sky. The air is motionless around me. I stand in my own little pocket. I am separate from the world. We both are. A few drops of rain begin to fall. I don't feel them. I fly into one in front of me. It splashes and slides off in the way it would over a car's windshield.

I try to stay close enough that I don't lose him, yet far enough that I won't overshoot him if he changes direction. It looks like he's standing in an invisible elevator that can move in every direction at will. We both look that way on the monitor at the top of the wall in front of Braxton.

A few of the others in uniform speak emphatically to those in the suits. It's too hard to focus on the conversation to know what they're saying. The whole scene plays out vaguely in my imagination, like a film dissolve frozen between one place and another. I need to keep the picture of myself and where I am first. That needs to be clear. If not . . . it's a long way down. I can almost cover the entire research facility with my head.

The name "Delgado" pops into my head like an idea. One of the military people must have said it. The two at the head of the table have two stars on each of their shoulders. The words "domestic air strike" come from someone else. I can't tell who and can't focus hard enough to find out.

A raindrop silently splatters against the emptiness suspending me in the air. Others follow. It's more than a drizzle now. The clouds above me look like a thick roof over the world. I spot Wendell there, maybe twenty feet up, eighty or so feet away. There's no glowing trail around him. He's stationary, focused on something other than movement.

I charge at him. The raindrops streak over me. I lean in and prepare for a collision. I don't know why I want to hit him. It could make both of us fall. I don't care. I want to smash into him with every bit of force I can. I want to knock him unconscious and watch him fall, even if it means falling myself. I'll take the son of a bitch with me. I brace for impact.

He startles. He shifts at the last second. I feel him brush past, actually feel him there, like I did when he clamped his hands on my face. The same contact that re-opened my connection to Eden. I stop quickly. He buzzes around again. Glow and water trails follow his every move. Rain breaks over the bullet-shaped pocket encasing him. I follow with my eyes. He's my mirror. Equal and opposite.

"Do you see them, Odin?" he yells across the distance. His voice is clear. There's no wind or rainfall to drown him out. The rain pours down in sheets. We are both completely dry. None of those things exist in my piece of the world. "Have you seen the fools and what they want to do?"

Braxton says nothing as the two generals nod to each other. A gray-haired woman in a blue pantsuit says something that I still can't make out. Or maybe I'm unwilling to try. She looks gravely around the room and then to the monitor. The rain breaking over us causes Wendell and me to stand out from the rest of the dull sky and the facility far below. She nods as well.

"After everything they have seen. After millennia

of ruin and death. They still believe more destruction is the answer. They would rather blow up their world than allow it to change."

The full crowd in the room bunches together to clear a path as one of the generals stands to approach a telephone next to a large monitor on the back wall. On the monitor is a topographical map of the continental states. Bright dots overlay the static image. Several such dots swarm just off the southern tip of Nevada. Where we are. The general says something into the old telephone. His words are an unclear whisper. His lips look like: "Authorized." Then I hear, "Take them out."

"Do you see them now, Odin? What they want to do to us?"

"If it'll stop you," I say, seething, "let it happen."

"What I have started cannot be stopped. It can only ruin their only chance at survival."

I laugh at that. There's a flash to my side. It's only lightning.

"The destruction. The panic. I know you have seen this. All that is left is to start again."

I steady myself for another charge. If there is a missile coming, the best thing I can do is pull his focus away until it explodes.

The rain pours through my view as I watch for any movement in the sky.

"Do you understand what happens if I am not here to accept their hatred?" he asks, perfectly clear even in the storm raging around us. "The true cause of today's calamity remains a secret. Its message will become twisted into justification for more and more destruction. Without a known enemy, they will lash out at anyone. Those they dislike. Those who are most convenient. They will find someone else to retaliate against. Then those retaliated against will respond in kind. On and on the cycle continues. I have seen this in every ruined world in history."

There's the faint sound of a scream in the sky.

"Unless they are given one simple answer. Me. Us. We did this. We did this to unite them."

I can't tell where it's coming from, but I know it's coming.

"One of us must survive or every sacrifice will be worthless."

He notices me watching. He turns. I charge.

I hit Wendell with my shoulder. He grunts on impact. I wrap my one functioning arm around him. I try to wrap my right arm as well. It does nothing but hurt. His limbs are bone wrapped in cloth. I try to wrap my legs. One of his gets free. His needle fingers dig into the back of my head. He scratches at my shoulders. It feels like dull razors scrapping through my shirt. I cling so tightly it seems as though his brittle ribs could implode between my arms.

The screaming is right in my ear. It's not the missile's scream. It's Wendell's. I picture myself impossible to move. Fixed in this place and time. He kicks his free leg against mine. He shoves his elbows at me. A gap grows between us. I only need to keep him here a few more seconds.

I raise my arm to wedge his head back. The missile's scream covers all sound. I feel his weight pull down. He slides from my grip. He drops. His eyes go dim. There's no contact. I see the vapor trail as the missile approaches, faintly through the downpour, hundreds of feet away, closer by the second.

After I die, Wendell will continue falling. He'll splatter on the ground. A puddle of smashed flesh and bone, like the people in Clarke, the people he murdered as "sacrifice." I imagine the walkway breaking over Kevin as he leaped onto his girlfriend. Never knew that asshole would have it in him to care about anyone more than himself. He didn't try to push her away or pull her onto himself.

I watch Wendell fall away. It's as if time has slowed to an eternity in every second. The way it was in Eden.

Dad went to the window as the light came. He

stared directly into the force that killed him. Mom dove under a table as she'd been instructed during the old bomb drills in school. Choi yelled for them to get under something. It was as though he had an idea of what was coming. Even Mrs. Moreland tried the best she could to save Andre. There was nothing any of them could do. They had to accept that which they could not change.

So have I. My conditioning, my capture, my exile, my return, even my failed attempt to stop Wendell's assault. These are all things I had no choice but to do. But letting myself die in order to beat Wendell—in order to "win"—is a choice. I don't have to accept that which I can't change. Not the way they did. I'm powerful enough to stop it. I can change it. I can rewrite fate.

There is nothing but the scream. I see the curve of the warhead as it nears.

Too late to move. Too indecisive. I close my eyes. I cover my head. I brace for impact.

Wendell crashes into me.

6

THE MISSILE EXPLODES. FAR FROM ME. I FEEL THE shockwave. There's heat from the bright orange flames. They cut through the gray sky. The fire diminishes as I fall away. The rain cuts through the vapor trail behind the explosion. Raindrops seem to hover in the air around me, moving at the same speed. I can't see where Wendell has gone.

He saved me. While I was deciding whether or not to save myself, he made the decision. For his own purposes, but he saved me nonetheless.

It would be almost poetic if I let myself fall now. All that effort to get me away from the blast only for me to then plummet. But I won't let that happen either. Not after everything else, everything which has already been lost. I won't let myself die here. And I won't let Wendell either. I'm not a killer. That's the difference between him and me. He can sacrifice others. I can't. Not even myself. He has the will to act. I don't. At least, not until now.

I spot the ground rising fast to meet me. I imagine myself as a meteor, shooting to the Earth from some other world. I am a soft center held by a hard casing. I see nothing but rocks and dirt. The ground breaks around me. I lurch forward from the sudden stop, sloshing around as though I'm sitting in an impenetrable bubble of water.

I look up to see rocks tumbling on top of me. They hang in the air over my head. Rainwater fills in every gap. It means he must have survived as well. That may have been my only chance.

He'll go back to the weapon. He probably already is going back. He could see through Burnett to find the facility's location from wherever he fell. He could have propelled himself up and away while I tucked and crashed. He has the will to do that.

He'll find his way back to the research center and storm through the hole blown in the side of the building. The machine is unusable for now. He'll learn how to repair it. In the wreckage could be the pieces needed to complete construction. Replacement covers are already there. Panels and wires are probably stored in some other building. He could find them among the torn-out guts and scraps. The big spools of wire should be fine, but the panels are more delicate. Still, he'd find a way. I'm sure of that. He always finds a way. I don't even have to guess any of this, I could see it up to a second ago. I just . . . don't want to.

Meanwhile, at the same time, I imagine Wendell is on his way to the facility. Braxton's crowd continued arguing the legality of firing missiles at domestic targets. They spoke of mass panic spreading through cities, military personnel being requested to hold back rioters, and the civilian leadership demanding answers that they couldn't afford to give. One of the generals pointed at Braxton and said, "If we still had firing squads, I'd put you in front of one right now." The monitors on the upper walls continue to stream images of the dismantled complex. The rain filled in the large gaps left from Wendell's work there. Some of the water seems to take on a slightly red hue. Everyone around the table yells at each other. I can focus on them now. I still can't understand a damn word they're screaming.

If I keep my head down, close my eyes, and hold this protective shell thick enough that it mutes the rain hitting the top, then it feels almost peaceful. It's a perfect black, the same thick darkness that I saw when I first arrived in Eden, before the possibilities pulled me away from enjoying my view of nothing. I've never had this before, not in the real world. There are no stars or streetlights or glowing clock numbers or green dots on sleeping electronics, only darkness and calm and peace.

Burnett heard nothing but beeps and static on the other end of the line. She slammed the receiver down on the old curly-corded telephone tucked in the rear corner of the computer station in the central building of the research center.

She dropped back into a seat in front of the active computer, the only one that hadn't gone to sleep since our arrival, and the only one that didn't require a password to wake it up. She opened a program labeled "Shell Mail" to find a textbox requiring a user ID and password. She opened another called "CORnet" to the same textbox.

She scrambled through the papers piled on the desk around her, tossing them off one by one after scanning for passwords, usernames, file locations, phone numbers, anything that could be useful.

She raced between the different terminals. She threw open the desk drawers and riffled so quickly through loose sheets that small slices appeared in her fingertips, none of which broke the skin. She pushed the papers off after flipping through, getting them out of the way in the fastest, most cathartic manner possible. The papers scattered on the floor behind the desk in the same way the rubble outside the computer station's window did; several clumps gathered around a central point. Through the many splintering cracks in the window, she could see the stillness outside, where Wendell and I had both abandoned minutes before. She no longer heard any pops or booms, no more gunshots or heavy artillery firing nearby. Quiet replaced the noise. She heard nothing but the weight of her own breath, the shuffle of paper and her feet across the floor, and her occasional muttering: "Okay," "Come on," and "Where are they?" as she flipped through every page she could, as quickly as possible, with no success. She slowly cracked open the door to the outside. She peered through the gap between the door and the frame to scan around the room and the rubble still contained within. There was no sound, no motion. She stepped out.

The dark made everything a murky gray. Shards of glass and rocks mixed in a solid line several feet from the window. Large chunks of material had collapsed on the floor. A hole was blown in the wall near the ceiling. Solar Flare was bent and broken in places, perhaps irreparably until help arrived, if it finally did. Delgado lay half buried in a heap of rubble. He stared at her. Lifeless.

She looked around, surveying the destruction and anything still left intact. Other than the damaged segments, Solar Flare seemed mostly untouched with patches of dust clouding the once shiny surface. Not functional now, but it would be soon. The rear of the room had only a few errant chunks of concrete wall flung into it. She couldn't see them but knew that the exits were blocked by the rubble outside. There was a soft noise like static nearby, then the patter of rain coming in through the hole in the wall. She stepped cautiously, as though too much of a rush would cause the ceiling to collapse on top of her. She moved around the machine and toward the far end of the room where the metal storage bins sat bolted to the floor. "Must be somewhere," she whispered, moving across the far end of the room.

She found more bins, all closed off. Another door, storage sign on the front, was locked. She puzzled at this for a moment. She leaned closer to the door handle, the long bar meant for pulling outward. Hinges were visible on this side, painted to blend in with the gray walls. She looked back at the rubble thrown around the room, then to the large rock that had crashed down on Solar Flare, denting two of the individual segments inward like a storm-tossed tree branch crushing the roof of a car. The rain fell harder now.

She moved to inspect the damage in the machine. The mass of wall scraped along the top of one segment before slamming to a halt at the edge of the next. She stood up on her toes and could barely see the interior through the gap that had opened up between the segments. She moved around the front, striding easier this time, feet clicking on the floor. The first of the segments was knocked crooked with another huge dent carved in from impact. About half of the outer rim was shredded. The shell of an unfinished segment was still wedged between the machine and the platform that kept it off the floor. She glanced inside to see where the internal wires bunched up and split from where they'd been pushed back. The initial impact knocked off or broke several of the internal panels. She took a long breath, exhaling slowly. A crash of thunder echoed through the room.

"This never should have happened," she said, staring skyward.

Wind now blew the rain through the hole in the wall. The water pooled with the dust, gravel, and rocks on the floor. The clouds were barely visible through the sheets of rain pummeling the outside world. Nothing but a gray haze was visible from where she stood. She heard another boom of thunder, but saw no lightning, just a rounded, foggy gray outside and a jagged, solid gray inside. Destruction in here, desolation out there. She took another long breath and stared out. She reached one arm across her body to rub behind her ear three times.

"I thought . . . " she looked down toward the pile of rubble where the rain fell. A few drops of blood mixed with the rainwater. She shook her head. " . . . I thought that we were building a better future. A new age of enlightenment and peace and," she chuckled, "all that idealist shit." She swallowed. "I thought . . . " She shook her head again, as though dismissing whatever it was she thought. "We betrayed you. We used our own science . . . " She glanced back, toward Delgado. He stared back, but not at her. "We were no better. And now—"

She became aware of a loud screaming coming from somewhere outside. She spotted the vapor trail among the clouds, a thousand feet up. Or maybe she didn't see the trail at all. She heard the explosion. It startled her. It silenced the noise of the wind and rain. She gasped as a ball of color broke the grayness of the world.

She closed her eyes and dropped her head. She said something silently to herself. She looked at the computer room window, the flat surfaces between the cracks. She marched back toward the door with the same resigned determination of a death row prisoner's last walk. She opened the door, closed it behind her, sighed, and fell into the chair. The computer had gone to sleep.

Wendell will probably kill Burnett when he gets there. Or no, he'll say that he wants her to live long enough to see the result of her research. He'll say that she started this project to find a way to use my power—his power—for her own good. He'll probably say "her" rather than "their." Instead he used the machine she built using him. He'll probably tell her not to feel ashamed for her failure. In fact, when these initial growing pains are over, she'll—she will—see that she has succeeded. She wanted to change the world for the better. That is exactly what she did. He will stand with his palms open to his sides like some kind of savior. *The result may not have been the way she expected,* he'll say. *No, it is so much more, so much greater than you could have ever imagined.*

The sky outside is nearly as dark as it was under the rocks. Overlapping shades of very deep gray mix into black where the clouds are thickest. The rain pours down as one mass from the sky. There is nothing but gray in the distance. This is possibly more rain than this desert has seen in years.

I push the rocks from on top of my bubble. I let the force around me dissipate. The ground beneath my feet is completely saturated. The water below soaks through my shoes and socks. The water above drops through my clothes and onto my skin. The impact even stings a little, especially over the cuts on my forearms. It's nice to feel again. Even pain is preferable to nothing. I hold my left arm out. The right hangs. The caked blood washes right off. Both cuts cross over most of the inside of the forearm. The one on my right arm is a bit wider from the angle of the metal that sliced it. Neither is cut is deep, just a few opened layers of skin and nothing else. Nothing that can't be healed. Everything can be healed, if treated correctly. Everything.

It's cold from the top of my head to the bottom of my feet. The pain through my arm is a dull, numbing throb until the smallest movement reminds me the injury is real. This is all real. This is real and solid and tangible. This is matter. This has matter. This matters.

I keep Burnett in my mind and close my eyes. I find her, then I find the weapon. I find the weapon, then I find Wendell. Hopefully in that order.

7

I HEAR THE WIND RUSHING PAST MY EARS. THE RAIN no longer touches me. It flies off in my wake. It sprays from my sides as though the drops themselves were forming a shell for me to run through. I keep Burnett in my mind as I zoom across the desert floor. Everything looks the same from down here: just gray and gray on top of dark brown dirt, saturated with a layer of gray reflecting the clouds overhead.

She's to the northeast, not too far away. It was hard to keep track of which direction I was falling after the explosion. It didn't hurt, but it was still quite a shock to witness. I wasted too much time feeling sorry for myself, immediately before and immediately after the missile strike. There may still be more coming. I need to get to Burnett fast.

Wendell is already on the way. I know it.

I see Burnett a moment before. She remained in the chair facing the computer screen. She held her forehead in her hand, propped up by an elbow on the desk. The network's ID and password prompt shut her out from the entire system.

There was a rumble outside the door. Shelves of copy paper boxes and computer equipment rattled against the wall to her right. The same wall continued beyond the computer room and into the main workspace. The rumble intensified. She looked just as a loud cracking shook through the entire wall. The vibration knocked a couple of the boxes and computer drives down from the shelves lining the interior.

I can't tell how far away she is. I see what looks like it could be the fence around the complex out there, several hundred feet away. It's hard to tell in the rain.

Wendell's already there. The rumble Burnett heard was him pulling the rubble away from the front of the Solar Flare building. He brushed them all aside as if they were those old foam bricks made to look like rocks. The cracking was him finding the seams left in the hole blasted into the wall. He opened up the splits in the wall and traced gaps in the exterior in the same way I did the asphalt in the road leading toward the building.

I definitely see the fence now. Most of it is still standing. Rolls of razor wire lace the top of both the inner and outer fences. Everything behind the fences still blends with the gray rain.

Burnett could barely make out what was happening behind the shattered glass between her and the large machine room. She heard the shaking. An entire shelf fell forward only a few feet from the first terminal. She ducked under the desk in front of her and curled up in the corner.

Outside, Wendell ripped the cracks from the punched hole, linking through the bullet holes like connecting the dots, all the way up to the ceiling and down to the large front gate of the building. He tossed his arm to the side. The wall snapped off as it swung open for him. The concrete gate remained lowered and unmoved, but now half the entire building facade was gone. It had been tossed along with the rest of the rubble. The rain water darkened the floor.

I don't even see where the front gates of the two fences have ended up. I do see the remains of the two fallen guard towers which flanked the entrance. Most of the other towers lining the internal fence appear to still be standing. The rumble inside starts to come into view. There's the squeezed tank. The rest of our destruction remains obscured in rain and distance. More of it becomes clearer by the second.

Wendell walked directly toward the entrance to the computer room. He reached one hand out and pulled the door from the hinges. He threw it out through the broken wall. He walked slowly around the other side of the desks.

Burnett closed her eyes, breathed quietly, and tried to make herself as small as possible in the little corner underneath the tabletop where the computer wires led to the outlet in the floor. She heard Wendell's footsteps as he slowly approached. Her eyes remained squeezed tight, as though not seeing him meant he didn't exist.

He pulled the chair out from her side. He sat. He looked around at the room at the papers strewn on the floor, the knocked-over bookshelves, and dented boxes. The sight made him grin. He bounced up and down to make the chair squeak from his meager weight. He folded his hands into his lap. He seemed almost giddy.

"Odin will be here soon," he said. "He is on the way now."

Burnett would have been able to see Wendell's

hands folded in front of him if her eyes were open.

"Only a few more minutes and then they can have this place." He squinted while staring at the fractured view of the room outside. The rain blew far enough in that even Solar Flare was starting to drip. "The machine is useless," he said. He glanced to one of the boxes that had fallen from the bookshelf. Several pens spilled out and broke on the ground. Nothing was immune from his destruction. "You know, I actually admire quite a few things you did."

Burnett winced while squeezing her legs in.

"The depth of your manipulation was . . . beautiful . . . in how effective it was."

Burnett repeated a whisper to herself.

"There was a time when you truly made me believe that this project could fix everything that is wrong with this planet."

There's the piled debris from the two buildings I clapped Wendell between. The few structures that still stand mix with the emptied husks of those torn apart. The bodies remain scattered all around, more camouflaged in the dirt, rubble, and rain than they ever could be while still living.

———◡———

"That cannot be a comfortable position for a woman your age," Wendell said. He pushed his chair back a few feet. "Come out of there."

Burnett shook heavily against the corner under the desk.

"You are not some peon, Doctor," he said. "You do not cower. You should be proud. You are an architect who made something infinitely more complex than anything ever built before: me."

She held her place.

"Come out now!" he screamed. The desk over her shook.

The rain gives even the shattered bits of rock and severed metal a slick shine. The twisted messes look polished and refined, like sculptures carefully arranged to appear natural. The bodies look waxy in the way they lay so still. They linger in my view as I speed past. Even the raindrops are stationary. I fly over the gap ripped into the road.

Burnett reluctantly slid out from her position. She stood upright in front of the desk. Her head turned down and away. She shook very slightly.

"All of this . . . " he said. She flinched as he stood up and walked past her. He motioned toward the room outside the window. "All of it, is because of you." He wandered back around the desk. She turned away when he stepped into her view. "Nothing to be ashamed of. No one can ever know the result of their creation until it is completed." He placed his hand on her shoulder. "It is okay. Even I had it wrong my first time."

Every part of her trembled. He took a step back. She refused to meet his stare.

"Look at me!" He screamed at her. She slowly turned to finally see him. The caved-in cheeks, the skin flakes clinging to his nostrils, the bulging eyes—yellow in the center like mine—the line of blood on his forehead, the veins running down his neck. "It is good," he said. "This is what the world needs."

There it is, straight ahead, with the wall torn open. The rubble of every building thrown aside to leave one big entrance directly toward what remains of Solar Flare.

"One thing remains left to do," he said. "Then they can have this place." He turned for the door.

I barely see him there. He's a thin, watery shape almost invisible behind the downpour. The rain cascades down and over and around me. The wind chills through my drenched clothing. No matter.

Evelyn's hair was still damp from her shower when she arrived at school this morning. It hung heavy down to the middle of her back. She hugged her binder in front of her. The green cover stood out against her purple sweater with the thick collar and the knit pattern that formed to her waist and stopped at her hips. She wore a black skirt that fell to just above her knees, black tights, and boots. The overall darkness matched the gray clouds in the sky that she looked toward as she walked, then to the trees, the last brown leaves still clinging on, and she sighed and continued up the path toward the entrance.

Some of the junior guys turned to watch as she passed the benches next to the door. One nodded approvingly as another snickered at her and a third shook his head. At the senior benches lining either side of the main hallway, she spotted Maria sitting between Calvin and Derek, a couple of baseball players. Maria waved as Evelyn passed. They hadn't spoken since Maria migrated over to a table near the back of the lunch room with a couple of the other party girls a few days ago. Evelyn got Brent and Richard to join her and the Drama Club girls near the front. Brent joked that Richard could follow Maria over there if he wanted. Evelyn laughed but told him he probably shouldn't try.

"So she *is* blowing both of them?" Richard asked.

"What?" Evelyn said, "No. It's nothing like that."

"Not what I heard," Richard replied.

Evelyn shook her head and waved her hand in dismissal.

On the phone with Brent that night she confirmed that she'd heard the same thing from a few of the Drama Club girls. "She's my friend," Evelyn said, lying down with bare feet hanging off the bed. "You don't say things like that about your friends."

She continued down the hall. She passed the classroom where we had physics last year, and Mr. Romero's class, where we sat and talked the morning before the fight with Kevin. It was the last conversation we had—the last we'll ever have—the day that everything started to change. She stopped at her locker near the last set of classrooms, before the intersection branching to the side exit and the cafeteria, and the rear staircases to the upper floor classes and the library. She spun the face of the big combination lock she'd had since freshman year: 24-6-17. I'd never cared to know that combination before. It doesn't mean anything now. She moved a few books from her bag to the locker. An old, red-covered copy of *Hamlet* remained near the front of her bag.

"Hey," she heard from several feet away. A few other students walked on as Brent neared them from behind. She offered him a little smile. Some of the puffiness in her cheeks was gone since the last time I saw her.

"Hi," she said.

Brent looked over his shoulder and hers. There were several underclassmen roaming around, but no teachers in sight. He put a hand on her hip. They kissed. She nuzzled his cheek. He ran a hand down her hair. She leaned away.

"Sorry," she said, "still not dry from the shower."

"It's okay. Smells nice."

She hugged her binder to her chest again. "I've been thinking of cutting it actually. At least before auditions start next quarter."

"You sure? It looks so good like that."

"It's kind of a pain in the ass. Takes forever to wash and dry. And it could get in the way on stage too."

"I still like it," he says.

"Maybe that's something I could do," she said, a hint of mischief appearing in the way she cocked her head, the gold flecks in her eyes and the reflection of the diamond shape at the tip of her nose. "I could cut it on stage. Like during the last performance." She opened her eyes wide, and with a a big grin, continued on. "When Ophelia goes crazy. Grab a pair of scissors, or a knife, and chop it off right there."

"I'm sure the janitorial staff will absolutely love that."

"I could carry it with me," she said, her eyes flashed wider as though she'd just had a brilliant idea. "Hold it in my hand and skip off stage with it."

He chuckled sweetly. "That would be a pretty crazy thing to do."

"Exactly." A big smile.

"Or you could skip along and throw it around like flowers," Brent said. He mimicked whimsically tossing things behind him. Evelyn laughed. "You could hold it up to your face," he put one hand on his chin and brushed the other downward, "and stroke it like a long beard."

She laughed loudly. Her eyes narrowed to slivers from the size of her smile. "I was just kidding, but now I kinda want to do this," she said as the laugher subsided. She seemed to glow as she looked at him.

"And when the performance is done, you could donate it to one of those hair charities after."

She frowned slightly. "And I'll feel bad if I don't."

"Nah," he said, scrunching his face at her, "I'm sure it looks better on you."

They both went quiet for a moment. They smiled pleasantly before looking away. She stared at some space behind his shoulder, behind even the lockers against the wall.

"You okay?" he asked.

She snapped back to attention. "Great," she said. She looked into his eyes. "Really great."

Light poured in through the entrance windows far behind him. She leaned to see. He turned.

I know what happened next. I don't need to see it again.

Wendell stole that moment from them, that moment and every other. Whatever happiness and sadness, glory and misery, triumph and pain, that this life—this individual life among all other possibilities—held from that moment forward was gone. All the things she didn't know she'd feel, experiencing in the moment without practice or pretend, she would never feel them. Because of him. He took everything. From her. From them. From me.

Only one thing remains.

8

WENDELL STANDS AT THE VERY EDGE OF THE FLOOR, balancing on the jagged lip where the front wall broke off of the central building. What's left of Solar Flare sits far behind him in the room. He grows larger as I speed toward him. He leaves his arms by his sides, hands hanging loose near his thighs. I lower my left shoulder, keeping my dead right arm back. He appears to inhale, ready to talk. My entire body shakes with rage. A primal scream begins in the back of my throat. It moves through my chest. The sound shoots out. No more throwing things. No more talking.

I want to feel his jaw crack on my fist. I want

to see the glow fade from his terrified eyes. I want to crush him into the ground. Make him feel the same pain, the same horror as they did—Ben, Aida, Choi, Andre, Kevin, Brent, Evelyn—I want him to see the end coming and be completely powerless to stop it. He starts to crouch. I hit him.

I roar on impact. Pain bounces up and down my arm like ripples in a small pool. I stagger backward. My momentum throws him as well. He crashes against the front of the machine. The staircase leading into the metallic tunnel crumbles into itself. His force appears to shove the platform under the machine back a few feet. The shredded first segment lifts off the platform several inches. It slams down.

I charge him again. Sloppy, I know. My feet never touch the ground. He dodges. I turn. A concrete slab flies. The air around me absorbs most of the force, but I still feel it. My entire right side is on fire. I spin to face him. He throws another piece of wall at me. I blast through it. I charge. He shifts quickly away. I growl in frustration.

He continues to move back, as though sliding across the floor. I stalk him until he reaches the broken edge of the building. The rain outlines the energy field around him. I fly at him again. Again and again as much as is needed. The rain slips over my head. I am a second missile, a heat-seeker, ready to explode on the target.

Chunks of broken concrete fly at me as I approach. I toss them away. I break them. I shatter them into dust. I follow him through the rain, watching the trail of water and glowing eyes as he shuffles side to side. I keep a steady pursuit. No more charging. No overshooting. Get close. Narrow that gap between his energy and mine. He could be luring me in. Go ahead.

I keep my teeth clenched. He told me to become a lion, a ruler, not a little boy, not someone else's servant or tool. I have become exactly what he wanted. And now he'll suffer at the hands of his creation, the same way he wanted Burnett, Delgado, and everyone else to suffer for creating him.

He's gray and painfully thin, a specter floating back and forth. He's a haunting, a remnant.

"This is what you want?" I hear no rain or wind. I only hear him, and the heavy, chest-heaving breaths moving through my nose.

"Is this how you want this to end?" he says.

This ends when he is broken. When he faces the edge of eternity with the same terror and panic that they did. I say none of this.

"Very well," he says, "one more time."

I roar. I lift every piece of loose matter within fifty feet. I swing my arm wildly, screaming. Everything I have launches at him. He disappears into his little bubble. I keep the pressure on. I squeeze my fist so tight the nails puncture the skin. That's what I want to have happen. I want him crushed on every side. I can feel his resistance fighting back, holding each piece of broken wall, office desk, table leg, chair, stapler, pencil, used bullet and bullet shell, everything that spilled out when he gutted the buildings of this facility. There are more objects than I ever thought the human brain could focus upon. None of it breaks through. The objects drop away as I charge.

He lunges at me. Our impact shoots through my whole body. I slip onto the ground. He leaps on top of me. His vein-riddled hands scratch as my face. I fling my arm out and catch him under the chin. I wedge my palm to wrench him away. One bony finger claws across my eye. I bring both my legs up and kick him off.

He pounces at me again. His open hands reach for my head. He's a zombie coming for my brain. I flail my legs at him. I stretch my neck away. I throw a haymaker with my one good arm. He dodges away but I make some contact. I actually make contact. He continues through.

His fingers seize the side of my head. He pulls at my ear. His hands are cold and stiff like exposed bone. He digs his nails in. He's trying to pull me closer. I stuff my hand under his chin again and shove him with all the strength I have. His fingers slip off my ear. My back remains on the ground. The rain pours down on us. There's a crack of thunder and the sky behind him lights up. He flails madly, scratching the air as much as me. His Adam's apple and every vein and bone in his neck presses against his skin. It looks like his entire throat could rip open. I shove his chin repeatedly. He grabs my outstretched arm to pull himself closer.

The world around us darkens. The clouds become a uniform gray behind him. The ground dulls behind me. A spark fires in the center of my head.

***

"Oh c'mon, use your jab!"

A boxing match is on the television. The fighters circle each other in the center of the ring. One fighter inches forward, limping slightly with every step. The other fighter staggers back, head rocking as he moves.

The television screen isn't as sharp as the rest of the vision surrounding it. The TV was old, one of the first things my parents purchased after their wedding. I remember this day. I was two, maybe three years old. Yet it feels like it's all happening in this moment, as though the past weren't gone. There is only now.

George, my dad, leans forward to the very edge of the couch. He presses all his weight through his elbows and into his knees. The couch is firm enough that I leave barely any impression in it. My feet kick the air and bounce off the cushion. White socks with red and yellow stripes on the ankle blur into solid streaks in the air. The coffee table is farther than I can reach. There are a pair of books near the edge of the tabletop. Their titles are indecipherable squiggles.

"C'mon! Get him!"

One of the fighters backs into the ropes at the far side of the ring. He has a small cut on his brow and some swelling under his eye. The other lurches forward, head moving in a circular motion. The bloodied fighter slides along the ropes toward the corner.

"Throw a damn punch!" George yells at the screen. He gestures with both hands.

"Yeah," I say in a little squeak. "Throw a damn punch!"

George flashes a huge smile at me, so large that his whole face is teeth. "That's it," he says laughing.

"Throw a damn punch!" I say again.

"That's right!" he says, swinging a fist in front of him.

"What are you doing to our son?" says a voice behind me. The room becomes a blur as I look around for where it came from.

"Showing him how to fight," George says. "Or to yell at the bums who refuse to."

Wendell's fingers tug at my locked elbow. He shifts around, trying to angle his chin free of my outstretched arm and open palm. His other hand clamps to the side of my head. He tries to grip. He scratches at the skin under the stubble from my last shave. I think of MacPherson at Colton. It was months ago for the world, years ago in my mind, days ago for my body. Wendell's head twists violently. I wish it would twist enough to snap. *Snap!* That would be fitting. I feel another scratch across my face, another jolt in my mind.

I see brick buildings with metal bars over the windows and colorful fliers attached to every door. Pedestrians tower over me, some looking down as they pass, others stepping away. Car bumpers and headlights blur behind them. I feel a tug at my arm, held up in the air. My birth mother, Rose, looks down at me, my little hand in hers. She smiles. "Almost there," she says in a sweet tone. My view of her face jostles heavily with my every clumsy step. "First day for Odin. Excited?"

"Yeah," I say in a tiny voice.

"Good. And don't worry about the other kids. It's their first day too. So they are just like you."

"I know," I say.

"You shouldn't be scared to talk your classmates. You could have twenty new friends by the time school is over today."

I don't say anything in response but I look up as she continues walking me on. I lose track of my steps and start to fall.

"Oops," she says, reaching down to pull me up. "You need to be very careful on the sidewalk. This is not a place you want to fall. You could get hurt or run into by someone else." She kneels down to make sure I am straight up on my feet. She stands as she asks, "Are you okay now?"

I look up and her and nod; her face and the sky behind her bob up and down with the motion.

I remember drawing a picture that day of big trees with long, twisting trunks and billowing leaves. The sun over them all had rays bursting out like my mother's hair.

I draw back to give one strong shove. His hand rips away from the side of my face. I kick at him to put more space between us. I scramble to my feet.

"You saw it," he says. "You saw them."

I clench my teeth again and heave with every breath. I keep one hand out while the other swings uselessly.

"How it was before the world changed."

I growl, "Before you changed it."

The world is a mass of watery shapes and dull colors. I can't focus on it. It's intangible.

He shifts around so quickly that he seems to

flash. He blurs back and forth. Glowing eyes trace from one spot to the next. I blink. He's on me. He grabs for my shoulders as though trying to pull me in. I duck away. I thrust an elbow out. His teeth snap together from the blow. I angle to keep my good arm forward and the other out of his grip. Every movement is pain.

I should be stronger than him. He looks like he could fall into a pile of bones. The cut on his forehead isn't bleeding anymore. The scar under his eye is barely visible. I still feel some of his scratches. They're little stings across my eye, ear, neck, and cheeks. I hold my only useful hand out in front of me. The cuts on my arms aren't bleeding either. My entire right arm throbs with pain. I should still be stronger than him. Yet he just keeps coming.

"Strange it would end this way," he says.

The rain bounces off him but doesn't seem to touch. It looks like he's wrapped in an extremely thin layer of energy. Not the big bubble. That must be how he's able to move with such strength.

"This is not like the last time," he says.

He flashes away. Grabs me. A searing pain shoots through my arm. Darkness closes over my eyes. He yanks the torn muscles and broken bones straight. I scream in agony. He grasps onto my throat. I choke.

I try to push him back. He twists out. He wraps his scrawny arm about my broken one and turns it around. The pain is everywhere. I hear nothing but my own choking cries. There is no ground below me. The world is a creeping darkness with a pulsing red intruding into the sides of my sight. His glowing eyes burn into me.

The blinking red light tells us not to walk. We weren't planning to.

We stand in the middle of the corner of the street as other pedestrians move around us. They continue on as though we aren't even here. They don't need to step away or adjust their movement at all. Instead, the world surrounding us functions so perfectly that our every move seems woven in with that of every other thing that exists anywhere. The pedestrians, the cars, the streetlights, the sun, the reflections of the sun, even one another, are carefully crafted to be so complementary that none of it, nothing in this entire existence, could possibly be real. This isn't real. I remind myself of that. Nothing in this world is real. I feel a squeeze on my hand.

Evelyn looks at me with a sheepish smile. The tip of her nose is angled slightly down and her big eyes, with their golden shafts, stare up. There are no stray marks, lines, or shadows anywhere on her. She squeezes my hand again, both of hers wrapped around mine.

"What are you thinking?" she asks.

"That building," I say, looking across the street and up toward the structure standing out among all the others. A tower of glass stretching impossibly high, it's a literal skyscraper. I point directly at the second window from the left on what I know is the twenty-fifth floor, but is so much higher. "We must look tiny to the people up there. Insignificant compared to everything else."

She wraps one arm around mine and leans to place her chin on my shoulder. The crowd continues to flow passed us, as though we were the center of everything else. In fact, we *are* the center of everything else. We are the eye in this perfectly ordered storm.

"So?" she says, looking up at me and nothing else. "So what if the world is bigger than we are? Means there's more of it for us to discover." She rubs her cheek on my shoulder. The other people disappear. "With you there's always more to discover."

I laugh happily, rubbing her hand in mine.

His every movement is forced. The arm locked around mine, the hand on my throat, the grimace, it's all centered behind the lightning in his eyes. He doesn't move from the inside out. He moves from the outside in.

The space around my bad arm is a tiny, microscopic cast. I picture that cast pulling my arm back. He wrenches my arm straight. Every nerve screams at me from beneath the skin. My mouth drops open in an agonized roar. I grit my teeth and try to black out the pain, before I black out from the pain.

Pain. Feeling. Sensation. Movement, all come from the mind. We don't think about any of these. We just do them. We make it happen.

I tear my arm from his grip. I force the elbow back. I picture the air around my fist as steel. I swing for his face. There's a solid, wet crack as my knuckles make contact right under his left eye, square on the thin skin between the lower eyelid and the bulging cheekbone, directly on top of the scar left from the last time I'd been hit.

They are all so tiny down there, billions upon billions of them. They move so blindly. It could be me down there—me with her, me with them—staring up at me looking down on them. On us. It feels like I have seen them all before, seen them all in one of the millions of worlds.

There are so many different people, different versions of the same people, all of them lost. All of them wandering helpless. They look at each other as enemies. They draw lines to keep them from the other them. Yet they are all servants of probability, equally trapped, equally disposable. And here I am, drawn behind the thickest of lines. Separating me and them, them and me. Even with all I could show them, I remain exiled, watching, watching it all over and over forever.

What am I watching? Is this Wendell? Is this Eden? There's the window. There's the entire world projecting out from it. None of this was real. It's a facade Eden built from my subconscious. What happens here means nothing to any world, any real world where any of the real versions of any of these real people will know, or feel, or understand what's happening in this unreal world.

What must that feel like, being of consequence? Being real? Being? How does the air feel on my fingers? They know how it feels. There is so much I know that they do not, and yet, even the feeling of emptiness across my skin—the simplest state of existence—has escaped me. I could change that. It takes only one moment to remember. Only one.

He staggers from the blow. I cringe. The hurt lingers from the back of my neck all the way down to the knuckles in my balled-up fist. He shakes his head. Blood drips from the wound. I must not have connected hard enough. I'd wanted to rend the skin from his skull.

I feel the ground under my feet. The force of the world holds me in place. The raindrops soak through my clothes. I see the ruins of the buildings and the remains of the work that took place within them. The fallen bodies nearly blend with the rest of the destruction, but I see them again.

"You," he growls, beginning to turn.

I launch at him. He shoots backward. I punch the air. He shifts side to side. His movement is stuttered and uneven. As much blood drips from his face as rain. His cheek is already starting to swell. I bob and weave like the boxers my father used to watch with me. *Throw a damn punch*, he would yell at them. I push myself left and right and then forward. I attack.

I hit a wall and stumble back several steps. He lifts his gaze to meet mine. His entire face is glowing behind his eyes. He brings his palms together in front of him. He presses them until the veins in his forearms rise as mountain ridges beneath the skin.

"One of us must survive," he says. "But just one."

I feel a shock in the center of my head. The spot we both have, the posterior cingulate cortex, which connects us to the energy. I know he's in there. I retreat several more steps.

I will send you back.

He draws his hands apart. A thick, eternal black stretches between his palms.

I have come too far.

The darkness widens in front of him. I feel it tugging at me. My shirt begins to puff outward.

Only one.

My head feels like it's about to explode from the inside out.

One alone.

The infinite dark stares at me through the tear stretching between Wendell's hands. A rip into the space between worlds, a single broken thread in reality exposing that which lies just outside the surface. The everything and nothing.

Wendell remains still. Every muscle and vein tenses in his arms. I continue to stagger back. Raindrops, loose gravel, bullets, and bullet shells pull from the ground and disappear into the rip slowly lengthening in front of him. The hole doesn't have the same pulling effect on him. He is on the other side of this black hole, beyond the event horizon.

The universe demands that only one of us be here.

My feet begin to slip. I search the ground for something to grab on to. The concrete is cracked enough to dig my fingers behind, but could also rip away at any second. Several bullet shells bounce off me on their way to the hole. I dig my feet in the best I can. I stretch as though trying to climb away from him. I duck as a broken table leg flies at my face.

This is how we save them.

I extend a small crack in the ground. The edges scrape against my cuticles as I squeeze the fingers of my left hand in. My smooth fingertips might make it harder to grip. I glance back. The tear is almost diamond-shaped, wider than my shoulders and more than half my height. The rain being sucked into the hole shows the cone of its pull. Outside, the rain hits the ground normally. It does behind, as well. I force my fingers to clamp down in the opened crack in the concrete. The energy field pushes so hard it feels like the bones could crack.

In my head, I see Wendell a second ago. He's trembling with the effort of getting this gap open. His veins bulge out as though ready to pop. The rain has soaked through his clothes and pours off of him. The rain touches him.

My left foot slips on the slick ground. I feel it being stretched. It's pulled toward the tear. The rain continues to fly as through blown by a hurricane. The space within the cone is clear of debris. Only

I remain. Outside, under the thick layer of rain, everything else is still. I locate the nearest piece of rubble, the back of an office chair. It's hard to focus on. I force my right arm to swing for it.

There isn't much force behind the seatback as it flies out of the dark, but it's still enough to knock Wendell to the side. The pull of the tear lessens. It requires his focus. If I can distract him enough, I can force him to loose concentration. Distraction causes objects to fall from control. Maybe the same will close the tear.

I make sure my grip is secure before tossing everything there is, much of what I'd thrown at him before. Broken wall, office supplies, lengths of copper wire, a soda can, a flat tire, more wall, I spot anything I can and launch it in his direction. Some of it disappears in the tear. Some of it misses wildly. He redirects a toilet seat flying for his head. The pull lessens more. I roll onto my back to aim. I launch more from all sides. Broken tree branches, parts of crushed vehicles, one of the soldier's weapons, if I can see it, I can use it, the bigger the better. But I avoid the bodies. There's something macabre in that. Finally, a five-foot chunk of wall flies. It's on target. He shields himself before the building side hits. The block shatters. The tear closes.

"Enough!" he screams. The shout makes the earth shake.

I rise to my feet. I place both arms in front of me. My right arm still burns but I force it to move. The rain stings on my cuts. I snort, like a bull preparing to charge.

"You will not hold me back, Odin!"

The wound on his cheek is the size of a golf ball. The glow of one eye has narrowed from the swelling. The cut on his forehead isn't bleeding at all. It could be scabbed or he could be holding it back.

"You are the villain here," he yells. "Not me! I want to save these people! You are trying to destroy them!"

I see Choi face down on the floor in my parents' dining room, Aida watching as his blood pools on the tile. Ben was torn apart by the shattered glass even before he was crushed. Aida's last act in this world was to curse me. Not him. Me.

"Do you understand what will happen without me?" He thumps his chest. The water splashes from his shirt. "The chaos that will follow if I am not here to stop it?"

I'd never met Mrs. Moreland but I see the inside of her skull as it pops against the staircase of Andre's school. Andre buried his face into asphalt. He was thirteen years old. Two months from fourteen. Two quarters from high school.

"Millions will die because of what's happening today—victims, innocents. The violence will be uncontrollable."

Kevin's first instinct was to try to save Whitney from the falling floor. First instinct, last action. In a less thorough destruction, he'd have been called a hero. His new school would have loved him for it, even more than they did before. His new life would have been complete, with no old scars or stories to follow him.

"Uncontrollable for anyone but me," Wendell says, no longer screaming or animated. The water running down is face is clear. There's no more blood mixing into the rain. He's holding the wound closed. "That is what you never understood," he says, pointing a sharp finger at me, "Sacrificing one to save thousands."

I think of the way Evelyn looked at Brent, with the shine in her eyes and carefree smile. It's the way I always wished she'd look at me. I don't know if she loved him then or if he loved her back. I don't know if they ever would. But it was their right to find out. Not mine. Not his. Theirs and theirs alone.

"They wanted you to be that sacrifice. I saved you from them."

If I look really hard, I may still be able to see Delgado half-covered in the rubble, eyes stuck open but dulled. Rogers looked sad as he fell away, sadder than usual. I wonder if he knew what was happening. I know McPherson didn't. I can see still him there, on the floor, reaching out with his empty hand. *Head twist. Snap.*

"I saved us. And I can save everyone else. Only lose a few. Those who are absolutely necessary."

Absolutely necessary, he said. McPherson was the first. He too was absolutely necessary.

"You are a ghost of a dead world, Odin. A fluke who never should have existed in this or any other life."

"And you still can't stop me," I say, staring at him directly in the half-glowing eyes. The pounding rain forces me to yell. "With all your power, you can't stop me. You can't kill me. You can't hold me. You can't control me."

I see his chest rise with a long inhale and fall with a longer exhale.

"I will always come back," I say.

He begins flexing his fingers in and out.

"Whatever you do. Whatever you say. I will always, always, *always* come back!"

The light from his eyes burns into mine.

"And you don't have the will to stop me!"

He doesn't move.

The first piece comes from my right, a ten-foot block from one of the buildings. I hold it back. The next piece scrapes the ground on the left. It's a block with "2nd floor" painted on it. I hold that back at well. Others come quickly and from all sides. They slam into each other. Half a dome builds in seconds. My right arm drops limply. More blocks smack into the field around me. I don't hear them hit. I see them block the light and the rain on every side. I am completely covered. I feel their pressure through the energy I picture around me. The matter inside my skull pulses. I close my eyes.

I see the formation enclosing me in the center. It must be at least fifteen feet high, twenty feet across.

Layers and layers of material press onto themselves and onto the empty air in which I shelter myself.

Wendell tenses with the effort. I see a blood drop forming at the corner of the line across his forehead. It's an open wound, an opening like a crack. I imagine the blood vessels under his skin, the tense veins in his neck. I hear the scraping of the concrete above my head, trying to get through. I picture the blood traveling through those veins, from his heart . . . to his brain.

I picture that blood stopping.

"Boom," I whisper. "Headshot."

He drops to the ground.

Everything drops to the ground.

9

THICK SHEETS OF RAIN ABSORB THE CRASHES AND thuds as the slabs around me fall or slide to the ground. I push the remaining blocks aside, releasing the energy that sheltered me in the process.

He's collapsed there, right where he was standing a moment ago, the same way Delgado did. He's fallen to the side, knees bent in front of him, right leg over and straighter than the left. He's slick with rain. I approach slowly, imagining the different ways he could surprise me. His eyes are closed. He's breathing. He's alive but damaged, with no way to tell how severely. There are some people who never recover from losing a second of blood flow to the brain. I place a thick field over him. The rain stops two inches from his skin. He should be trapped inside.

I lean in for a closer look. The dim light clings to the sharp angles of his caved-in cheeks. He's all harsh lines and thick shadow. I can barely see his eye through the swelling. His arms are twigs wrapped in meat.

"Odin?" I hear under the heavy pounding of the rain. I turn to see Burnett's orange jumpsuit like a beacon in the gray world. She strains to look at me through the rain.

"I'm here," I call back to her.

She looks up and sighs at sheets of rain still pouring from the sky. She crosses her arms and steps through the wall that's half torn off the front of the Solar Flare building. I look back at Wendell again. He's almost tranquil curled up like that. I hear Burnett's wet footsteps approach.

"He's alive?" she asks.

I nod, not taking my eyes from him. I look

closely and see the many lines on his palms, those I lost when I returned and those I acquired while running from Choi. It feels like a lifetime ago.

"How?" Burnett asks.

"I gave him a stroke."

She looks down at him. She puts a hand over her brow to keep the rain away.

"My god," she says. "I didn't know you were able to do that."

"I don't want to be."

She kneels for a closer look. The skin on Wendell's face is as tight as that of a corpse. Will I look like that someday?

"A stroke," she says, "does that mean he'll—"

"I don't know, but he won't go anywhere. I have him contained."

She reaches a hand out. Her fingertips contact the edge of the energy over him. She flattens her hand against it. "It's like . . . a wall at the end of the world."

"You saw it before."

"Not like this," she says. The rain begins to slow, just a little. "There's no give or texture or anything. It's like nothing exists there."

I can't stop looking at him, lying on the ground, curled up and harmless. He is the monster that lived in my mind, took over my body, and destroyed my life. He destroyed everything I'd ever known and cared for—my birth parents, adoptive family . . . no, just family, even Aida, Mom . . . my little brother, everyone I had called a friend, everyone I wanted as . . . more than a friend. Evelyn would never get to be Ophelia. I won't see any of them ever again because of what he did, because of what I allowed him to do.

There are gaps in the raindrops, but still enough to mask the tears forming in my eyes. "This is because of me," I say.

Burnett turns to look up at me. She pushes the wet hair from her face.

"Everything that he did. Everything that you did. Delgado, Braxton, Choi, all of Solar Flare.

The whole city." My voice quivers. "Everyone I care about. Because of me."

"No," she says, standing. "No, no, no." She reaches to put a hand on my shoulder.

I step back from me.

"None of this was your choice."

My lip shakes. My fingers twitch. I look around at . . . nothing. There's nothing I want to see right now. There is nothing that doesn't remind me of the destruction.

"You only wanted what was best. I know you do. Remember?" she says, again trying to reach out to me. "I know you."

I see her eyebrows up. The lines in her forehead are more pronounced than I'd ever seen them before. So are the lines under and around her eyes.

"The clouds are starting to thin," I say.

"What?" Her brows lift in the middle.

"Construction crews have reached the edge of the city. Where the road ends. They want to begin clearing the rubble, in case there are any survivors."

She frowns.

"There aren't any. They know there aren't, but they don't want to say it."

The rain slows to a drizzle. Except to breathe, Wendell is still motionless on the ground. "Emergency workers have branched off in every direction. They step carefully to avoid any . . . remains. They're still far from my neighborhood. The roads are cracked, the sky is filled with ash. Even if they found anyone alive, they wouldn't be able to help them."

She draws in a long breath and shifts her view away.

"There's a water main break at the corner of McQuarrie and Singer. The water is higher than anything else in the entire city. No one is there to see it."

A wind sends a shiver through my whole body. Shaking makes my arm hurt.

"They're all gone," I say. "Everything is gone."

She turns to me again. "Not everything," she

says, shaking her head. "No. No, no, no, not everything." She changes to nodding. "We can recover."

"It's over."

"It's not," she says, eyes huge with desperation . . . confusion . . . excitement. I can't tell which. "It's a new beginning."

I look away from her.

"Yeah," she says. "Don't you see it, Odin? It's the start of a completely different world. We can build from this." Her speech quickens. "The world will see the consequences of abusing this energy. They'll know that it should only be used in controlled and monitored situations."

Hints of light reflect off the water dumped on the ground.

"It'll be everything we talked about. Entire cities on self-contained, unlimited grids. Electric cars. Space Travel. Maybe even levitation and movement without any energy at all." There's a mania to her voice. "The technology is here. It can work. We can still make it work."

I shake my head. "It's too much."

"I know, but it's a starting point. You never know where research may le—"

"It's too much for anyone to control." I look at her. She wears hope and madness in equal parts. "No one should have this type of power."

"We can, Odin. We can learn to use it for everyone."

"It'll become a weapon. She'll become a weapon."

"Not anymore. Not again."

"Yes. Again. There is always an again. Always."

Her hope disappears. It's replaced by resentment. The madness remains.

"As long as the temptation of power exists," I say, "there are people who will use it for themselves."

"You don't get to decide that, Odin."

Dad, Mom, Andre, Evelyn, Brent, Kevin, Richard, Choi, my classmates, my neighbors—their last moments were terror, unknowing terror. Their final memories of this life are panic and loss. They will never know anything more. They'll never know what killed them or why. They'll never have a happy ending.

"No one can take this away, Odin, not when we're finally so close. When everything we've worked for, everything we've sacrificed for, is so close."

"Sacrifice," I say. It's the same word in the same voice that Wendell used.

"That's right." The soft curves in her forehead have changed to harsh cracks in her brow. "As horrific as what happened in Clarke is, what happened to the people there, it has been done. You can't change that. The best we can do is use their sacrifice for the good of everyone."

"Sacrifice," I whisper, "what do they know of that? They're dead. It doesn't matter to them if we recover." I glare at her. "They won't see it. They won't see anything."

"We can at least work for their memories," she replies. Her eyes narrow.

"And what about the next time?"

"Then we do it again!" she yells. "We try again and again until we get it right. No matter how hard it is, we keep trying. That's how humanity works!" The lines in her face have gone sharp and deep, not like Delgado's, but not the way I used to see her. "And you don't get to change that."

The concrete beneath us is a light gray. The clouds must be almost gone now. Wendell remains on the ground. The little finger on his left hand twitches.

"Again and again," I say quietly, "until we get it right."

"Exactly," she says, calming. "We can salvage this." She places her open palms in front of her, as though pleading. "We can find a way to make this world work."

"You're right," I say. I close my eyes. I breathe out slowly. "We can make this work."

"I'm glad yo—"

I appear in my mind myself exactly as I was a moment ago. Water still dripping from my chin. Broken arm hanging. Cuts on my forearms. Scratches on my cheek, ear, and over my eye.

I hear myself speak. "Until we get it right."

Burnett says something. It fades into silence.

I see myself the day before. I sit at the dining room table, talking with my parents. I stare down at the table as I speak. There I am before then, on my knees in my bedroom as Ben—Dad—holds a gun on me. I show him the smooth tips of my fingers.

I'm at Colton now, walking through the underground complex in the orange jumpsuit and the thin slippers. Rogers opens the door to leave the common room. He and McPherson follow behind me. My head is freshly shaved. I have a scar under my eye. The scars on my hands blend with the lines which were already there, along with the ridges on my fingers. There was a bruise on my ribs which healed shortly after I arrived.

I'm in the school cafeteria with Choi, the last day of my previous, normal life. There's the short hair I'd always had until then. I hold a napkin over the cut under my eye.

Sitting in the hall in front of Mr. Romero's class, my knees up and forearms across. Evelyn is next to me. My face is a little more childish, a little rounder and without the scar I'd get and later lose. I felt so much lighter. I never did find out what her totally awesome birthday present was. Probably best not to. Not now.

There I am sleeping, reading, bowling, eating with my family, eating with my friends, talking on the phone with Evelyn, with Brent, with Kevin. I'm fighting on the basketball court after school, and racing Dad into the water after being told not to, and lying under the tree in the backyard looking through the leaves overhead, and sitting on the curb with my oversized backpack telling a new friend about the old friend who talks only to me, and playing Chinese checkers with Burnett on the big couch in her office with my little feet hanging off, and walking into my new home for the first time with eyes large from wonder and sadness and hope, and seeing Wendell for the only time standing there, like me but smaller and less clear. I'm stomping through the apartment building lobby and out the door to the curb, with the traffic only feet away.

I find every second from this one until my first. I hold all of these moments in my mind at once, all of these different versions of myself. They merge as though every second of my life were happening right now. There is only now. I keep that image in my mind.

Then, I remove it.

10

FEELS LIKE I'M OPENING MY EYES AGAIN FOR THE first time.

There is no mass of lights to greet me. The twisting, branching shafts that once overwhelmed all of Eden are gone. In their place is nothing. The dense, black nothing of oblivion. Then, a few lonely points appear.

The jumbled, overlapping paths of the past nearly touch the hazy ceiling of the future. Between them is only a short span of time, like a sapling just big enough to move from its pots to the soil. I erased everything between them. Small as it is, this shaft lights up so brightly that it stands as a lone beacon in an eternal dark.

I knew that completely removing myself from my world would have consequences. I'd hoped that it would serve as a reset for just that branch of existence, allowing everyone else to carry on without me as they did in countless other worlds I'd seen my last time here. I didn't expect the result to be like this, the one tiny speck of life in an infinite emptiness, a squat stump of present existence, the past fading until forgotten, and a future that can never be fully seen. There are no other possibilities, only this one, the world of the anomaly.

I turn away from the world. I lower myself to sit on the ground. I don't feel anything below me but I know it's there. I stare at nothing. My shadow would be projected outward if anything other than darkness were there. The familiar vibration begins in my head.

"Hi," she says, as light and friendly as ever.

"Hello," I reply as she appears in front of me.

We're almost the same height with her standing and me sitting. Her closed-lip smile makes her cheeks big like a squirrel's. She has the same ears that stick out from the sides of her head, same large eyes with their painted-on pupils, same plaid dress and white turtle neck sweater. I figured her appearance was how I imagined her, but maybe this is how she imagines herself.

"What's your name?" she asks.

I blink for a moment thinking she should remember me. But then, there is only the present here. I erased the world where we had met.

"It's okay," she says. "You are welcome here."

"You don't remember me, do you?"

She looks confused. "I've never met anyone like you before."

She didn't remember me then either. I guess, without a consciousness here, she doesn't retain any thought of her own. It's a whole new life for her.

"Odin," I say. "I'm Odin."

"Nice to meet you, Odin. I'm Eden."

Maybe in collapsing my world, I disconnected it from all other possibilities. That could be why no others exist. In trying to keep from destroying one world, I could have destroyed infinitely more. I hang my head.

"Nice to meet you too," I say quietly to the only . . . person . . . I will ever speak to again.

"Why are you sad?" she asks.

"Because . . . "

She waits for an answer. She doesn't breathe. She doesn't blink. She watches, patiently, forever.

"No reason," I say, trying to look as pleasant as possible. "I'm . . . happy to be here."

She smiles.

Staring at darkness forever becomes old, isolating, and depressing very, very quickly. So instead of looking into the emptiness, I build.

I build what I know to build. I build from my memory with nothing else to look back on. I build the world as I once knew it, the time and place that doesn't exist anymore. I create rules for this world: gravity, oxygen, physics, the rules of form and shape that dictate life as I have always known it. Feels like it takes decades to put it all together. Eden helps, using my knowledge to fuel her energy. Together we build a world vaster and more detailed than anything I could do alone. Then I erase. We build again, over and over, a hundred times over. The world is never right. The people in it are never right. There's too much. These worlds we create are too big or too rich, too bright or too dark, too vast or too limited, always too something.

"It's not right," I say, looking through the window I placed to watch over the construction. It's about the pots of dry dirt on the rooftop across the street. The clay isn't the correct shade of faded burnt orange. "It's never right."

She rolls her eyes at me, as she does every time I insist on starting again.

I allow the window, the room, and everything outside of it to break apart until all that's left are the growing columns of possibility. Eden's purest form.

I see the column of my world again, the real world, the world I came from. The gap between the past beneath me and the future above me has stretched exponentially since I began my exile here. I don't know how many years it's been for them, and I don't want to know. I don't want to see them. I can barely even remember what the world looks like.

Other possibilities have also begun, taking root from the threads of the past and growing in unison with each other. Seems like every time I begin again, there are more and more, each one ever taller than the last time I saw them. Time inevitably flows forward. New worlds are created every second, splitting off from each other, merging together, beginning, ending. Eden builds these on her own. I just want to make one.

I begin again with something small: the window. The glass goes first, a mixture of transparent and reflective. Next is the office containing that window, the four walls that surround it. The larger items of the room come next: the desk, the couches, the chair, the bookshelves. Then I fill in the empty space with books, games, finger paintings, the computer monitor, and the pen on the desk. Finally, I add the details, whatever I can remember on my own. Eden fills in the rest of the gaps that lay dormant in my subconscious. From there we would craft the street below and the world beyond that.

I sit down in front of the window. I place my hand on the glass. I see Eden reflected in the partially transparent wall, sitting on the couch facing the small table where Burnett and I used to play a board game, or something like that, all those years ago. Or maybe we'd just talk. I'd never seen what

Burnett had been like in my or any other world. She was the last vestige of the life I left behind. I remember how her face was during those visits we had in the real world version of this room. She would probably look like that now, or a couple of years younger. I lean toward the glass until the blobs behind it begin to form into familiar objects.

I see worlds where Alice Burnett never goes into psychology or neuroscience. She studies literature instead. She takes part in anti-nuclear protests in the nineteen seventies. She decides to take a year abroad in Spain and switches her major upon returning to later teach English there. She studies only psychology without neuroscience, and vice versa. She drops out of school, works as a waitress at a diner, is nagged by her parents for not applying herself and letting her intelligence go to waste. She dies in a drunk driving accident while out with the boyfriend who in some worlds becomes her husband.

I continue watching. I see worlds where my

birth parents, George and Rose, never meet, meaning they will never die in an accident together. In some possibilities George wins his first professional fight. In just as many possibilities he loses his first fight. In others he has to drop out while training due to an injury. In some of these worlds he meets Rose while running in the early morning, or at a party with mutual friends whom they do or don't meet in other worlds, or they bump into each other outside of a movie theater, him almost knocking her over before he catches her on the way down. Sometimes she's there for the few fights he has, sometimes she isn't. In some worlds, he quits boxing to support her through school. In one world she leaves him after an argument where he perforates her eardrum with one right hook and he later throws himself from the roof of the apartment building which they had moved into only three months before. That world never breaks through the past.

I see Ben and Aida as well. Ben marries while

in Korea and stays there. Aida never applies for the office assistant job that leads to the two of them working together and eventually dating and, in some worlds, marrying. Or she decides to study painting instead of international relations. Or he dies during a North Korean shelling of the DMZ and she contracts an extremely rare form of flesh-eating bacteria, and neither live long enough to meet. Every possibility has its own changes, events, personalities, histories, and outcomes, with infinite variations from the same starting point. But then, some don't even have the same starting point. I begin tracing the roots back farther, the roots that eventually sprout for me. Hundreds, thousands of years of societies rise and fall. Rise and fall, sure as the tide.

I see wars in every world, each possible outcome shaping the future in ways both grand and minis-cule. I see hundreds of lives, all of them their own little sparks in eternity, end in the same second. The fates of thousands in a war zone decided by a small group of men in a secure room hundreds of miles from the conflict. I watch soldiers in gray-green uniforms instead of the old grayscale of war documentaries. The soldiers fire brown guns at other green soldiers to spill red blood. I watch countries fight with each other and with themselves over a line on a map drawn by those who have never been among the people who live between those lines. I watch three generations of humanity be exterminated because they didn't worship their god the way others did. I watch a crowd of civilians gassed and beaten for being wrong: the wrong color, or the wrong gender, or the wrong religion, or simply being in the wrong place at the wrong time for the wrong reasons. Children no older than I was stuff guns in the waists of their pants to walk across the road and to the next block where they're shot for wearing the wrong colored shirt. Women have knives held to their throats, or worse, for turning down the wrong alley or turning down the wrong man. I see scientists, "scientists," try to change eye color by injecting toxic chemicals directly into a prisoner's pupil as guards hold them down and force them to watch the needle go in. The birds in the trees of uninhabited Pacific islands disintegrate into nothing from yet another bomb test. Long ridges of dense nature burn instantly black as fire from chemicals mixing with oxygen rains down behind newly-built airplanes made to carry more weapons than any created before. I see a wristwatch frozen forever as an entire city is leveled. Tens of thousands of people—women buying food for the night's meal, men beginning their work, children starting their first classes—die in a second while the less lucky continue in agony, eventually succumbing after long decades of choked breath and tumors, blinded from skin melting over their eyes, limbs dying one by one before they do, fingernails growing up instead of out, begging the rest of the world to listen to their stories instead of building more bombs exactly like the one they wish had killed them decades ago. I watch as all of this is done to people at the whim of other people. All of it destructive. All of it chaotic. Yet all of it preventable, if they only knew better.

Even with all the other changes, every dissimilarity between the different worlds, these things remain constant: war, exploitation, violence, murder. They're so prevalent, so far-reaching, that even a sporadic occurrence—the one bombing in fifty years of peace, or the one shooting in a full year for another otherwise safe country, or the one foolish strike in a perfect marriage—drowns out all the good that happens every day. No one remembers the acts of decency, the geneticists curing diseases, the national leaders who negotiated peace instead of drumming up war, the community construction crew that drills the well that delivered water for an entire village, but they all remember the one maniac who sewed the body parts of a dozen corpses together, the general who sent families to internment camps or gas chambers, or the invaders who burned that year's crops to torment those who depend upon that yield to survive. In the end, the villains live forever. Kindness is never remembered. Evil is never forgotten. The only lessons learned are those taught through destruction.

"What're you doing?" Eden asks as I lean back from the glass after peering into yet another world of random slaughter and misery, where I saw a small cadre of people condemn those outside their group through some claim of divine right. In reality, they were all equally low, all flukes of probability in a universe more vast than their simplistic understanding could allow.

"I'm learning," I reply.

"About?"

"Humanity." I press up against the glass again. The dark shapes coalesce into the figures of men in hoods holding torches. They wrap a rope about another man's neck, loop the rope over a branch, and pull, or they wrap the rope about the other man's ankle, loop the robe over a car bumper, and drive. Either way, the result is the same, as is the cause. Hate. Fear. Anger. They, these people, are so blindly ignorant, so unaware of themselves as specks in a larger universe, that they hardly register as existing at all. Yet they claim themselves superior to others because of a belief or a color or a gender or wealth or standing or simply because they have the means to kill. It is disgusting. And it is eternal.

I wish that I could intervene with these people. Remove those who wish to do harm from those whom they wish to harm. I want to show them how much one choice, how taking the left path instead of right, could change not only the scenery on their way home but the course of their entire lives. Maybe, if I could somehow show them how small they are in relation to everything else, they would understand their place. They could work together the way other forms of life do, each contributing through a sense of purpose and place. No more questioning. No more fear. No more hate.

But I can't. All I can do is watch and watch and watch.

I don't remember when Eden stopped talking to me. She doesn't even come to this room anymore. Sometimes I can feel her there, vibrating in some long buried part of my mind. She continues expanding. She's pushing back the boundaries of eternity. Of course, none of her work will mean anything. The result is always the same. The individuals may be different, but people, the people who occupy these worlds, they never change. Not without some kind of influence. Not without a reason.

I was one of them once. I lived in one of these worlds. I walked amongst these people, spoke to them, interacted. I lived like they did, before I brought myself here, what feels like centuries ago, for some reason that escapes me now. Something about control and loss, betrayal and captivity. Instead of continuing in that life, I chose this exile. The world I left was flawed, hopelessly flawed. That is how I remember coming to this place. What is it like being one them? Being so limited? So finite?

I must be a toddler in these worlds by now. Now, the present, in every world where I exist. If I try hard enough perhaps I could find myself in one of them. If I can remember what I look like, if I could keep the image of myself solid enough, then there is a small chance I could find myself. It's been so long since I have looked at what little still remains from my time before here, a time equal to hundreds of years in which I have experienced tens of thousands in total. Did I ever even have a life of my own? Or have I always been here?

Perhaps if I could find myself, I could reach through him to touch the world, just for a second. I could feel one little slice of existence, the air on my skin, the ground on my feet. I could feel the sun on my face and hear a voice, any voice, vibrating the tiny bones in my ears. It would be just a minute, a second, a sliver of sensation. It has been such a long, long time.

My window beckons. I picture myself as small. I had dark skin and hair that made my light eyes stand out. I had a round nose that I used to stare at. I was thin too, especially as a child. So few details remain. I picture the earliest things I can remember instead—a staircase leading down to a room of blue and white tile, mailboxes along one wall, a heavy door with a bars over the window. The darkness begins to take shape.

There. I can feel it. A force. A little hint of pressure. I close in on it, feel it in every nerve. I make it everything. It's so tiny, so real. I focus on it even as it pulls away. No. Hold it there. Make it stay for as long as it can, for every second you can never feel again. Forever.

There is the window with the bars. There's movement behind it, close movement. Close but blurry. Shaking. Something is trying to throw me away. It wants to keep me from entering this world. It does not want me to have this one moment. It wants every moment for itself. It is okay. I will give it back everything it wants. One blink and I will leave. Leave myself, my tiny, possible self.

I will never interfere with him again. Just let me have this moment.

Please.

I hear it, the ambient buzz of life in steady beats of footsteps and waves of sound vibrating. It's a feast of sensation. They try to elude me. I concentrate on them, pull closer to them.

The shapes are poorly defined and uncertain. No. They are moving. They are shaking so much that clarity is lost. I straighten out, focus, come so close. I do not let this moment slip away.

"Odin?" says a voice, high and sweet, with a hint of casual concern. Is that what I am called here? Odin?

There is still a blur. Streaking shapes of color.

"Odi . . . ou a . . . ight?"

I hear the high, sweet voice again. There is something so familiar to it. I feel my hand, both hands. One is being squeezed. The other one is not. It shakes through the air. The air is on my skin. A weight pulls me down. Gravity—such a wonderful thing. It holds the world in place. I must steady against it and remember how to stand. I feel another shake like an electrical shock. The world is trying to pull itself away again. Not now. Not when I have come this close. I take hold while there is something to take hold of. I remember what it is like to cling so tightly that I feel the blood pumping through my fingers.

There are cracks in sidewalk, lines, gray concrete, black shadows. There are green patches between gaps in the sidewalk, white paint on the curb before the jagged black road. People rush by. Their footsteps are explosions compared to silence.

The man in front of me has a nose that is flat and familiar. Must be my dad. He reaches for me. His big hands are full of creases and channels between thick pores. His long, black eyelashes twitch as he blinks. I feel his hands on my shoulders. I want to curl up into that contact, wrap myself in it so I never forget again. There is another motion through the blur. I see a pair of eyes like mine.

Mom, with the high and sweet voice. She steps away. Her brow creases deep and thick within the skin, heavy with worry. If I can focus, I can stop the shaking. I can take it all in.

"Odin?" I hear my dad say. His face is a blur of eyes and noses and—I know this moment.

"No." I say this, say it into the world. My dad grips my shoulders. My mother steps away. "Not here."

I have to stop this. I must have control right now, absolute control. I pull into the moment. Every part of my body must be mine. I make myself straighten in the world, make the shaking stop.

I feel totality flatten against me. My father lurches forcefully forward. This is how it started before. I have to get out. I have to release.

"Not now. Not now."

Too late.

I see energy in the air. It ripples from me. My father is shoved back. My mother is as well, too far from him. She falls screaming. Dad turns to reach her.

This is the change. Rose—Mom—falls. George—Dad—pivots. The truck screeches and skids. It does not stop.

Mom hits the ground first. The truck rolls over her. Dad's head smacks against the silver grill. The metal shines through the blood. He bounces to the ground.

They are both dead before the truck stops. One tire rolls onto the curb. The driver stares wide-eyed at where they both disappeared.

"No." Must release.

The driver's knuckles are white with pressure.

"Not this." Must get out.

There is a scratch on the bottom of Mom's heel.

"Not now." Let the light and sound fade into nothing.

Dad's arm hangs off the curb.

"Not again." I let myself go numb.

The silver grill of the truck shines around the red splatters.

"No."

No. No. No.

Why?

Why did I have to do that?

I should have just looked, made sure it was a different time, any other time. Any time at all. I never should have gone back. I sent myself here, sent myself here to protect them, protect them from having this happen, happen all over again. Over and over again.

Nothing to do now but watch. Watch as he, as I, sit in the hospital, waiting for the news that he will not even fully understand until days later, in the foster home with three other boys asking what happened. He will feel so unbearably alone and trapped in a world that was not meant for him.

It does not last too long though. It's only a month before a man appears, a tall man with broad shoulders who introduces himself as Ben.

He says he will take care of him, take care of Odin. Odin does not ask why or where they will go. He just goes with Ben—Ben, the man who claims to be his father. It is the beginning of their lie. The beginning of the calamity which brought me here. I came here to protect them and yet, they will do it all again. They insist on destruction.

He, the real Odin, will need someone to guide him. He will need someone to help him see through the lies the world has for him. He will need to break free of their limited understanding. Then he can guide them himself. He could be the one to show them how different and special their world truly is, that they do not need to be afraid or angry or hateful. But it will need to come through destruction. Those are the only lessons that are truly learned.

There must be a way to reach him. I can make him see how different he is, how unique, how he can help change the world. He and he alone can free them of the evils they visit upon each other.

Even if this is the only world affected, this one can be different. This time it will be different. It has to be. I can guide him. I can show him the truth. I can teach him how to become what he is meant to become.

I will reach out to him. Guide him. Teach him.

I picture a time when he will be most accepting. The first day in his new home, when everything is unknown and he has nothing to do but adjust. There he is, the door opening in front of him. The woman is holding a little boy in her arms. There is the old couch and the old television. Speak to him. But not in his mind. That would be too jarring. Wait until he is alone so the others cannot hear.

It's hard to remember what I look like. He is too far to see in detail. How tall is he? Copy the rest from here, the eyes, hair, skin, the shape of the nose and face. Leave everything else blank. Be welcoming, so that he will want to speak with us.

There he is, everything he has ever known is hanging so low from his shoulders that it nearly touches the ground. I remember them enough. His new father, the captor who will dictate how he sees the world, motions for him to enter. His new mother, the one whose deception will last his entire life, smiles. She holds the new little brother in her arms, the poor child who will never grow to be worthy of anything except pity.

"Hi, Odin," she says in fake sweetness. "Welcome home."

He takes in the room, and the overwhelming newness of it all. He feels uncertainty and unknowing. He looks at me. I must welcome him, show him that there is nothing to fear. I must remember that he is a child, look at him as a child, speak to him as a child.

"He's probably tired," the man says. "It's been a long trip from Atlanta. He probably just wants to see his room."

Follow him. Find a safe place to talk.

"Does that sound good, Odin? You wanna see your room?"

How little he knows of what his future could be.

"All right, come with me."

Little Odin. This is not the only time he will follow. He pauses just outside the door. Everything is so foreign, including him.

The room looks so huge to him. There is a big bed on one side, a drawer of folded clothes, and an open closet with a chest of toys. There are bright and clean walls, as unblemished as he is. Everything they think he would want. Everything to make him listen to them, to mollify him into accepting their lessons, their plans. The same plans that made their world so flawed that I had to leave it.

"This is yours," the man says. "Everything in here belongs to you."

It never did. Everything always belonged to them. Everything inside this room, and everything inside him. They owned it all. They use it to make him into their puppet.

The boy waits for the man to leave. "Open or closed?" he says.

"Open."

"Good." Of course it was good for him. Easier to watch. Easier to control. "Welcome and get some rest."

At last.

Do not push him. Do not scare him away.

"Hi," I say.

"Hi," he says back.

He should not be here. If it weren't for me entering his world, and him being there when I entered it, he would be in his real home. Not here. Not with them.

"I'm sorry," I say.

He looks confused. Of course, he does not know what there is to apologize for. He never needs to. Not this time. I can help him. Things will be different. I can show him how to make this world different from the others, to make this the one world among billions in which the chaos ends.

But not yet. Do not push too much. Guide only. Make him believe he is the one choosing.

"What's your name?" he asks.

I need a name. Not Odin but something familiar. I had a friend long ago. Before coming here. What was his name?

"I'm Wendell," I say. I think I knew someone who was called that. I think he was one person who understood me. "What's your name?"

"I'm Odin," he says, confident in that fact.

Of course you are. You always have been. And I will be here to guide you.

It will be different this time.

It will be different.